For Tali
Buo

Abbracci e aloha
Margo Sorenson
(Maren's grandma & your
parents' friend) 😊

Secrets in Translation 😊

Fitzroy Books

Published by Fitzroy Books
an imprint of
Regal House Publishing, LLC, Raleigh 27612
All rights reserved

Printed in the United States of America

ISBN -13: 978-1-947548-20-6

Cover design by Selene Studios
Cover image copyright © 2018 by ronnybas, Shutterstock

Although set very specifically in Positano, some of the
places and all the characters and events in this story are
entirely fictitious and no resemblance is intended to any
real person, either living or dead.

Regal House Publishing, LLC
https://regalhousepublishing.com
www.fitzroybooks.com

Library of Congress Control Number: 2018939696

For the Adorables: Carson, Maren, Samantha, and Taylor

Chapter One

I could hardly wait for the disaster that my parents had planned for me this summer. No, you guessed it—actually, I could have waited forever, but my doom was not going to be postponed. An awesome, hoped-for, dreamed-of week in Tahoe with my new American friends and maybe even the chance for a hot boyfriend was gone, *pouf*, destroyed—all for my worst nightmare come true. That Tahoe trip would have been the perfect beginning to my senior year of high school in the U.S., but, instead, I'd been drafted as a summer nanny for the tween from Hell, in Italy, where I used to live. I cringed.

Everything *would* have been so perfect—the Tahoe cabin with my new friends, the special fun stuff to do arranged by my new friend, Morgan, and maybe even an American boyfriend—until this nanny problem exploded into my life. I could still see Morgan's shocked face last week when I'd told her I couldn't come.

"But, Alex!" she protested. "We've had everything all planned—Emerald Cove, Incline, Cave Rock—and we needed to have six girls to be able to go on the horse backpacking trip! Now, we can't go, and it'll be really hard to get anyone else this late to come for the whole week. And how about the guys from school coming to meet us for boating on the lake and barbecue after?" I had no answer. My heart sank.

Then, she added, "Besides, I thought you were done with Italy. You keep saying you're American now." Did she look at me sideways, or was it just my imagination?

I swallowed hard and pushed that conversation to the back of my mind. It had happened a week ago and I still felt awful about it. And now, I was stuck in the car with Mom and Dad, going to meet the family I'd be living with for six dreaded weeks.

Dad pulled up in front of the Cowans' house. "*Ecco!*" he said enthusiastically. "This is going to be fun!"

Fun? I wanted to groan. The three of us had been invited to dinner at the Cowans' to talk about logistics and to generally get to know each other, a plan which applied most specifically to *moi*, since I didn't really know the Cowans except to say "Hi." Carrie was the one I was really worried about. Mom used to come home from work at the college and tell me stories about the latest craziness that this Carrie had created. It sounded to me like her parents pretty much let her run wild. Great. Just great. Me in Italy, in charge of an international incident just waiting to happen.

Of course, because I'd grown up there, I knew there were lots of potential problems for a nanny and a wild child in Italy, as there were in most places. We'd all heard the usual media stories about Italian guys going after American girls, pinching their behinds and all that. But worse than that were the Mafia, the N'Drangheta, the Camorra, and all the other organized crime syndicates that existed below the surface of everyday life in Italy. Besides, if Dad's investigation into the Mafia influence in American wineries wasn't dangerous enough, I knew, just like everyone else in Italy, that the syndicates were involved in extortion, money-laundering, counterfeiting, drug-running, sex-trafficking, lots of violence—and definitely murder. And what about Carrie? What could happen to a pesky, rowdy, twelve-year-old running loose in Italy? And *I* was supposed to be her nanny?

"*Ciao!*" Mr. Cowan greeted us with a big grin, opening the door with a flourish. I bit my tongue—it sounded like "chow"—and smiled politely.

"Hi," I said. No way was I going to be forced to speak Italian unless I absolutely had to. I was living in the U.S. now, and I was determined to be just like everyone else, no matter what some snarky people had been saying at school.

"Alessandra," Mom said, "you know Mr. and Mrs. Cowan, don't you?" I nodded obediently. They looked eager and somewhat clueless, which I had kind of expected, given that they had raised a hellion like Carrie.

"Yes. Nice to see you again," I said politely. After all, I wasn't raised in the Diplomatic Service for nothing.

"Alessandra, we're so happy you can come with us and be a companion for Carrie," Mrs. Cowan said. "And please call me Nicole."

"And I am Phil," added Mr. Cowan.

I wanted to say, "And you can call me Alex," but I knew this wasn't the time to raise *that* issue. Really, all I wanted was to be Alex, the American, not Alessandra, the girl who grew up in Italy for almost all of her seventeen years; the girl who thought eating dinner at ten at night was normal; the girl who could pronounce correctly the name of every dish on an Italian menu; the girl who was so polite and formal with adults she didn't know, to the hilarity of her new American friends. I was doomed almost from the first moment I opened my mouth in my new American high school. So I quickly learned to keep it shut.

"You need to meet Carrie," Nicole said. "Carrie! The Martins are here! Please come and meet them."

"Carrie?" Phil called, loudly. Silence. They both looked at us and shrugged.

I already knew I was in big trouble for the next six weeks, because in my family, if guests are coming, my presence is required at the ETA, not texting my friends, not reading in my room. This Carrie needed to be actually called, and she was definitely not cooperating.

Nicole led the way to a comfortable family room. "She'll come in a minute, I'm sure," she said. "She's probably on the phone with her friends."

"How about a glass of wine?" Phil asked my parents.

Wine was served. I had Diet Pepsi, because who knew when I would next be able to get that treat? And so general college faculty and winery chat began. I tuned out, but kept an eye open for Carrie.

"Where have you been?" Nicole scolded, when Carrie finally appeared in the doorway. I didn't want to stare, but

I caught the low-riding jeans, the skinny top, and the pout.

Carrie looked up from her cell phone—she must have still been texting someone—tossed her red hair back and said, "Hi. I was doing something important. Sorry."

From the corner of my eye, I caught Mom and Dad exchanging a glance. Good. Maybe they'd rethink this nanny thing.

"Carrie, this is Alessandra Martin. She'll be your companion while we're in Italy, since Ingrid had to go back to Sweden," Nicole said.

Carrie looked me up and down, and I could feel myself bristling. Who exactly did this kid think she was?

"Uh, hi," she said, looking back down and moving her thumbs over the keypad. She must have pushed "send" because she put the phone in her pocket and walked in, plopping herself down on an ottoman. "You mean, nanny-babysitter," she said.

"If that's what you want to call it," Phil said, with a sigh. "Your mother and I will be busy working on our books, and we thought it would be more fun for you to have someone closer to your age to do things with, instead of being cooped up with us in the apartment."

Carrie shrugged. "Whatever. I don't want to go away and not see my friends for six weeks, anyway. I told you. So, it is what it is. Six weeks of total boredom while you guys do your brainiac stuff with your books. That's been the story of my life." She leaned forward, her chin on her hands, elbows on knees.

Nice, really nice, I thought. Of course, I felt pretty much the same way. After all, what I really wanted was to be with my new friends in Tahoe, setting up a great senior year. That chance was over. I held back a sigh.

"Italy is beautiful," Mom said in a hopeful tone. I could almost see the rose-colored glasses perched on her nose. "You'll love it."

"A lot of girls would love to go to Italy for six weeks," Nicole added. The earnestness on her face almost made me wince. Sure, they would—if they weren't trying to make new friends in a whole new place, working on fitting in and being like everyone else.

"It was lucky for us that friends of the Martins know the LoPrestis, owners of a local restaurant in Positano, who were able to find us a nice apartment to rent," said Phil. "That was very helpful." Carrie didn't look convinced. I wasn't either.

"Time to put the meat on the grill," Phil said, getting up. As if they'd been pulled up like marionettes by an invisible hand, the four adults got up, holding their wine glasses, and left the room. Their voices echoed back from the kitchen, the women's laughter rising above the men's deeper voices. Something must be awfully funny, I thought, but what it could possibly be, I had no idea. I didn't think anything was funny right now.

Carrie had pulled out her cell phone again and was engaged in texting. I decided to wait it out and not be pushy. Nothing I was going to say or do was going to change her mind, that was easy to see. I sighed. I couldn't believe this was happening to me—stuck with a brat for six weeks in a place I so didn't want to be.

I stood up and walked over to the bookshelves. The Cowans had tons of history books—Italian history, French history, English history. Then there were anthropology books—stuff on Easter Island, Africa, Polynesia, and big books on weaving and textiles. Nicole must be some kind of a retro-eighties macramé person. If she was that squishy and fuzzy and a wanna-be-back-in-the-day hippie, no wonder Carrie was like she was—not that I liked to generalize and stereotype or anything.

"What are you looking at?" Carrie's voice made me jump, and I turned around.

"I just like to see what people are reading," I said, deciding that the truth was probably the best answer when faced with attitude.

"Are you some kind of really smart person?" Carrie asked. "My parents said you read tons of books and you speak Italian like a native, which you practically are."

"I'm an American, just like you," I said, maybe a little bit too defensively, but no kid was going to put me back in that place I did so not want to be. "My dad was working for the U.S. government. I had to learn to speak Italian because everybody else spoke it."

"Did your dad go after the Mafia?" Carrie asked, scooting forward on the ottoman. "Was that what he was doing for the government? Arresting Mafia?"

I almost wanted to grin at the thought of my quiet,

unassuming dad, strapping on a Glock and taking on Italian organized crime face-to-face in Italy, but the truth about what he was doing was uncomfortably close to what Carrie had suggested.

"Uh-uh. He mainly bailed drunk Americans out of jail."

"Oh," Carrie said, her face falling. "I was hoping it would be kind of like those old movies, *The Godfather*, the *Departed*, the *Sopranos*, something."

"Well, the Mafia, and the Camorra aren't any movie; they're definitely real." Carrie's face lit up expectantly, so I had to crush her enthusiasm. "But I don't think we have to worry about it. Especially where we'll be, in Positano," I answered. "It's not like Napoli." I honestly didn't know that for sure, but it seemed like the right thing to say.

Carrie sighed. "The Mafia! The Camorra! I'd just like a little something to happen that would make these six weeks not so boring." She looked sideways at me with a half-grin. "How about you?"

I tried to hide a smile and shook my head. Twelve years old and she already seemed to be up for pretty much anything. Unfortunately, it was going to be my job to handle Carrie, so I thought I'd better try to set up some boundaries—as if I thought they might actually work.

"Well, when you're in a foreign country, you have to really watch it," I said carefully. This was a lecture I had heard so many times that I could say it in my sleep and probably did. "You have to remember that you may be one of the only American teenagers"—I gave her a big break here, because twelve is technically not a teenager— "some of the Italians may ever see. So, it's kind of important to not offend anyone."

Carrie frowned. "You sound just like my parents." She got off the ottoman and marched into the kitchen. I sounded like her parents? And that wasn't good, seeing how much respect she gave *them*! At least we'd sort of had a conversation. Maybe this kid wouldn't live up to her advance publicity but I was going to earn my pay, that was for sure.

After dinner and small talk, we said our good-byes and got into the car.

"Alessandra," Dad said. "We need to talk about the Mafia and the Camorra."

"What?" I asked. "What's wrong—what do you mean? Is it too dangerous for me to go to Italy after all?" My heart lifted. Was I home free?

"No, Alessandra," Mom said. "We heard you talking with Carrie about the Camorra and the Mafia and how they weren't really problems."

Nice. My parents were eavesdroppers.

Dad continued. "Lately, I've been finding out that there are, unfortunately, even more wineries and distributors in Italy under Mafia and Camorra control than we had thought. It's becoming clear that it's not going to be too difficult for those thugs to get into the wine business in the U.S. with threats and intimidation, as they're doing in Italy."

"Well?" I said. "What does that have to do with me?" Hopefully a lot—as in, now I wouldn't have to go.

Mom said, "It means that you need to remember the

Camorra and Mafia are everywhere in Italy. And there are many ties between Italy and the U.S. in the wine world. So you have to be very careful."

"Then why are you letting me go?" I asked, crossing my fingers. Could I get out of this trip, after all?

Dad chuckled. "You'll be fine. We're sure of that. Positano is out of the mainstream of organized crime. Besides, it is what it is in Italy, and you know how everyone just puts up with the Mafia and the Camorra. It's part of life there. But we only want you to be aware that it can't be taken lightly, no matter what you said to Carrie."

Mom, turning to look at me in the back seat, added, "It's fine to tell people who ask you that your father works for a winery in California, but don't say anything about organized crime, not even to the Cowans and especially not to Carrie."

"Duh!" I said. "You don't think I'm that stupid, do you?"

Silence from the front seat. Mom and Dad exchanged glances.

"Well, this does sound a little scary though," I went on. "I just don't get it. Why don't I just stay home and go to Tahoe with my new friends, like I'd planned?"

Mom sighed. "Dave, help me out here please."

"Alessandra, it's only cautionary," Dad said. "We've spent too many years in Italy and in the Diplomatic Service not to be careful about things like this, so just relax and have a good time. The Camorra and Mafia probably don't know that I even exist, much less that I'm working with Ralf's winery and looking into all these winery takeovers. They're not going

14

to make any connection between you and them—and they wouldn't bother with a teenager, for heaven's sake. They operate in a whole different world."

I leaned back against my seat, already dreading the coming six weeks. Organized crime or not, I was in for trouble any way I looked at it—with Carrie and with Morgan, and her group at Sonoma High. When I came back from Italy, could I still fit into the group as "Alex,"—the name I'd asked all my new friends to call me—instead of Alessandra?

With a sigh, I remembered how at first, at school, it had been fine, and even kind of special, to be "the girl from Italy." Lots of people at school thought being from Italy was glamorous and very cool and asked me lots of questions about what it was like to live there, and how cute the guys were, and, at first, everything seemed to be working. I made the tennis team—thanks to my Italian tennis pro, Guido— but didn't try to jump right into Morgan's popular group, even though some of the tennis team girls I knew were in it. I sort of hung around after practice and before lunch, pretending to be doing something else. After a while, Morgan or one of her friends would say, "Why don't you sit with us?"

I was so, so careful to wear the right clothes, to say the right things, and to be friendly and upbeat and have a sense of humor. But I started noticing jealousy amping up among some of the girls because of the attention that I was getting from guys. Then, to my complete shock, the Mean Girl comments started. One afternoon while we were all sitting at the cafeteria table, one of the girls I hardly knew spoke up...

"Oh, look! Here's Alessandra, and now all the guys are going to be coming around—all for her hot Italian-ness!" I'd had to back off the Italy thing, and fast. I so did not want to be tagged as "the Italian" anymore and risk losing my new friends, especially Morgan. Nothing was worth that. It was all about fitting in and being just like everyone else, and that was absolutely fine with me. If only I could really make it happen.

Why couldn't I be more of the rebel type and simply refuse the nanny job? I asked myself again for the hundredth time. Because I was not a rebel, I was now stuck for the summer, going back to a place I knew I didn't want to see again, ever. Rebel? That was so not me, and now I would be paying for it. Crossing my fingers for luck, I promised myself that spending six weeks in Italy wasn't going to make me any more different than I already was.

Five days later, I sat in the World Club, waiting for our flights to Amsterdam and then to Rome, remembering my stupid optimism about being able to deal with Carrie. I'd kissed my parents goodbye, promised to email them on the Cowans' laptops—since it was too expensive to call or text on my cell phone—and I had my passport, and my bag. I had everything, except excitement and anticipation about the next six weeks; what I felt was more like dread.

I sat next to Carrie in the WiFi hot spot lounge, trying to read my book, while the Cowans worked on their laptops and Carrie talked on her cell phone and texted with her friends.

She sat with her back to me—as if that would prevent me from hearing her squeals and shrieks.

So much for conversation with Carrie, but actually, I was fine with that. Her conversations seemed to be pretty much the usual seventh-grade "He said what?" and "She did what?" and I couldn't pick up anything that sounded like real trouble, just a lot of attitude. She was contained at the moment, as they say in counter-terrorism talk, or so I guessed, and my job right now was easy. Easy—except for the growing worry I felt about going back to Italy.

What would it be like? Would I feel a complete stranger after having been gone for almost six months? How much Italian had I forgotten? The Cowans were counting on me, I knew, and not just to be Carrie's nanny for the summer. They knew a little Italian, but they spoke French, mostly, so I was tagged 'it' for interpreting.

Worse, there was the big problem of organized crime and Dad's job. Even though my parents had smiled at my worries, saying I'd be safe in Italy, I still couldn't forget they had warned me not to let anyone know what Dad was doing undercover. To be extra safe, I probably should shut up about his even working at a winery. A feeling of dread seeped through me.

"Oh, my GOD!" Carrie squealed and began laughing hysterically. "No! You are kidding me!" she shrieked. Three other people in the lounge looked up from their laptops, frowning at the interruption. None of them were Phil and Nicole, still typing away, oblivious as usual to what their darling daughter was up to.

"Do you mind?" a woman in a navy suit asked in a cutting tone. Carrie actually heard her and scrunched up her face in reply. I hoped I didn't look related to Carrie. Her long red hair didn't look anything like my blonde short cut, and her freckled face hadn't yet lost its pudgy baby fat. I sincerely hoped mine had. My friends always told me I was cute, but I thought my nose was a little too turned up.

Time to start earning my pay, I thought, cringing inwardly. "Hey, Carrie," I said in a low voice. "There are people in here trying to work. Keep it down."

The look she gave me could have stopped a train. "You're not my mother," she snapped.

"You're right," I said. I wanted to add, "Thank God," but knew better. "But you've got to be quieter."

"You're going to be a lot of fun on this trip," Carrie said, turning her back on me again and, thumbs flying furiously on the screen, began texting one of her oh-so-lucky friends. My face felt warm and I hoped no one had overheard our exchange. I hated to be dissed—not that anyone really loves it. Maybe people could see that Carrie was, as my parents would say, "quite a handful," and ignore it. If only *I* could ignore it. Right. The Cowans were paying me to *not* ignore it.

What else was going to happen in the next six weeks to ruin my life?

Chapter Two

"Welcome to Rome's Leonardo da Vinci airport," one of the flight attendants announced. The plane landed, bumping a bit as we braked, and we coasted to a stop in front of the jetway. Like it or not, I was back in Italy. My mouth felt dry and I took a gulp from my water bottle.

The flight had been pretty quiet from LA to Amsterdam and from Amsterdam to Rome. Carrie had slept most of the time and listened to music on her iPhone, and the Cowans had read or worked on their laptops when they weren't sleeping. I listened to my music, too, and tried to sleep, but my heart kept pounding as thoughts chased each other through my head. When I did sleep, I dreamed in Italian, just as I had the last few nights before we left. Dreaming in Italian was just weirder than weird, and I hadn't told anyone—most especially my parents.

I'd not heard a word from Morgan or any of my new friends either. I felt awful just thinking about facing them after the summer. Morgan's disappointed face flashed in front of my eyes. What would I say to them when I came back? Six weeks seemed longer than forever. I knew I should email them from Italy just to keep in touch. I sighed, thinking of my best plans and hopes for finally being able to fit in during my senior year, crushed.

I looked through my mini-dictionary on the flight from Amsterdam just for a quick refresher for phrases like "please check the brakes," and "the tire is flat," in case my brain froze up, which it had been known to do under stress. If this wasn't stress, I didn't know what was—playing nanny to the twelve-year-old from Hell, and probably having to watch over her clueless parents, not to mention my worries about being called to interpret for six weeks. Lots of Italians spoke some English, though, so it wasn't as if I'd be totally on my own. I hoped.

I decided to email my old school friends from the years we lived in Bari—Caterina, Maria, and Giuseppa—even though it seemed unlikely that we would be able to see each other. Bari was all the way across the peninsula and they were busy with their studies, even in the summer. It would have been fun to get together. Well, maybe something would work out. Then I sighed, remembering that, of course, I was being paid to nanny the tweenager, not to hang out with my Italian friends.

We gathered up our carry-ons and made our way off the plane to customs.

"Look! Look at them!" Carrie exclaimed loudly, pointing up. I had already forgotten. Up above us on ledges, all around the airport terminal, stood uniformed guards, the *polizia*, rifles pointed directly at us—the passengers. I had become so used to seeing the police above my head in Italian airports that now I hadn't even noticed them.

"Are they looking for Mafia? For terrorists? The Camorra?"

Carrie asked loudly.

"Shhhh!" Nicole whispered, grabbing Carrie's arm and hurrying her along through the terminal.

"Carrie, be quiet," Phil urged her.

"Seriously, Dad!" Carrie exclaimed, ignoring his request. "They're aiming the rifles right at *us*!" At this point, I probably wouldn't have minded doing the same thing myself just to get her to be quiet. Now, people around us were staring and frowning. There had been too many attacks and threats here at Leonardo da Vinci, or Fiumicino as many Italians called it, and the Italians didn't mess around with security.

We managed to make it to customs without any international incidents, though the stern faces of the *polizia* stared down at us with narrowed eyes. Hopefully, they'd seen many girls like Carrie over the years and figured she was just another stupid American kid.

In the customs area, we stood in the non-EU line.

"We're not Eeeeu!" Carrie said, making a lame joke. I saw a woman behind us smile. Did she think we were sisters? I hoped not.

Phil and Nicole fussed with getting their passports out. I handed mine to the official behind the plexiglass window and waited. He thumbed through its well-worn pages—I'd gotten my last passport two years ago and it already had plenty of stamps.

He looked quizzically at me and asked in heavily-accented English, "You are American—but you have lived here? *Perché?*"

"*Sì!*" was the first thing that popped out of my mouth.

Then, in response to the guard's question, "Why?"—"*Mio padre ha lavorato per l'Ambasciata Americana.*" My dad worked for the American Embassy.

He actually smiled—a little. Customs guys were notorious for lacking a sense of humor, so this surprised me. "*Benvenuta, signorina,*" he said.

Welcome, miss. My first welcome back to Italy. If only he knew how much I didn't want to be here, maybe he wouldn't have been so nice.

The bomb-sniffing, drug-sniffing dogs passed us, the customs guys passed us and our luggage, and I guided the Cowans through the airport, following the green signs to the EuropCar counter, where Phil had rented a car for our six weeks. I couldn't figure out why we were going to need a car the whole time, especially when most of Positano had little, winding streets, some for pedestrians and motor scooters only. The town would be difficult to drive through, but that wasn't my problem. We Americans don't like to be car-less, I guess.

"Alessandra," Phil said, looking up from filling out papers at the rental counter, "would you mind just hanging around, in case this man has any questions?"

I stood nearby, hoping that nothing would come up. Thank goodness, the guy spoke English and I did have my little dictionary marked at "automobile," just in case.

Carrie slouched against a wall, her face in its habitual pout—an expression that I was quickly becoming immune to. In another line, I saw some young guys, Germans, from the looks and sounds of them, waiting to rent a car. One of them had noticed Carrie and I could tell that the three of them were making comments about her. Her jeans and top could have been from any country, but not her shoes, and her attitude was definitely American. That was going to be another problem for me, once we got to Positano—the guys. Mom and Dad had given me the "Watch out for the Italian Men" lecture before I left. They weren't so much worried about me; they knew I could handle myself, but they were concerned about Carrie. I was, too.

Walking to our car, we passed a news kiosk. Large, black letters jumped out at me and I stopped. Today's edition of *Corriere della Sera* had a huge, bold headline: "*Nuovo blitz contro il camorra, 11 arresti a Salerno.*" I glanced ahead at Nicole and Phil, but they were oblivious, threading their way through the crowds. There was a smaller headline underneath. "*Produzione d'azienda vinicola é distruggito.*"

Carrie looked at me. "What are you staring at?"

"A headline," I said, not wanting to translate what it said for her. I'd read silently, "A new blitz against the Camorra; eleven arrested in Salerno." My mouth felt dry. Salerno was the biggest city near Positano—sure, around the end of the gulf of Amalfi, but we had barely arrived in Italy and already I was reading about the Camorra. What was worse, though, was the smaller headline. "Production of winery destroyed." This was exactly what Dad had been talking about—the Camorra threatening and intimidating winery owners so they'd sell out cheaply and at a big loss.

"What does it say?" Carrie asked.

"The Pope is blessing the animals," I lied. I jerked my head in the direction Nicole and Phil had gone. "Let's catch up to your parents."

"Why is that such a big deal? The Pope blessing the animals," Carrie asked. "Your face looks funny."

"Thanks," I said. "Not a big deal and we're going to lose your parents, if we don't hurry up."

Carrie grinned. "Now that would be awful, wouldn't it?"

My heart was thudding in my chest. Wineries and the Camorra. Not a good combination. Actually, a dangerous combination. Please, let it all go away and have nothing to do with Dad—or me. I glanced back over my shoulder at the kiosk, almost wishing I'd bought the paper, but deciding it was better to just ignore the headlines.

"Come on!" Carrie said, in an annoying tone, as she pulled me with her. She probably didn't want to get lost in the airport without her parents, in spite of what she'd said. I took a deep breath and picked up the pace.

It was unsettling to hear so much Italian around me, and I tried to fight a creeping feeling of dislocation. Because I looked so definitely American, people didn't realize that I understood almost everything they said.

"D'you know what they're saying, Alessandra?" Carrie asked, after a young Italian and his girlfriend had walked past us, gesturing and arguing loudly.

"Maybe. Not sure," I answered, not liking the "Alessandra"

part. I had told her to call me Alex and she wasn't doing it. I could refuse to answer her when she called me Alessandra, but Phil and Nicole called me that too, so it would have been useless. It looked as if Alessandra was here to stay, like it or not, but I'd have to be on my guard to make sure that my name was the only thing to be changed in these six weeks. I was determined to blend right back in when I got home.

We loaded our bags into the Volvo Phil had rented, made sure the air conditioning worked, and we were off. This was the tricky part. Mom and Dad had coached me on how to get from the airport to what is called the ring road that circles Rome, and then the exit for the Amalfi Coast. Reading the signs was easy, and I could sense the Cowans' relief as Phil navigated the car onto the *autostrada* and headed for the Amalfi Coast and Positano.

I watched the landscape whiz by and tried not to flinch when Phil had near misses with cars zooming up behind us and swooping into our lane—it is true what they say about Italian drivers. My feelings churned as I looked out the window at the hills dotted with olive trees, the occasional random, crumbling castle, the tiny villages clustered around an ancient church bell tower, and the AGIP gas signs.

Unhappily, everything I saw through my window reminded me that my new American high school existence was fragile and uncertain. It seemed now as if I had never left Italy, and I didn't want to feel that way. I'd worked too hard to get to where I was now, back in the U.S. with my new friends—at least, I hoped they'd still be my friends when I got back—to let everything be destroyed by an unwanted trip back to Italy.

"Dad?" Carrie asked, jolting me out of my reverie. "Can we stop and get some more bottled water?"

Nicole and Phil exchanged glances and looked back at me. A sinking feeling began to spread inside me.

"You can't wait till we get to Positano?" Phil asked. "It's only another two hours."

"Please, Dad," Carrie repeated.

Nicole turned around in her seat. "Alessandra, where can we get some water?" she asked.

"Ummm, in one of those gas stations we passed—the AGIP. They have convenience stores in them," I answered. Maybe they'd just have Carrie go in by herself, or Phil would go with her. I was not excited about finally having to use my Italian on my own trying to get something done. Until I did, I was hoping I could convince myself that I was still really Alex.

Phil got off the A-1 autostrada and pulled into an AGIP. The familiar sign with the impassively staring, yellow she-wolf seemed to mock me.

"Alessandra," Nicole said, "would you mind going in to get it?"

I couldn't refuse. Swallowing hard, I answered, "Yes, uh, I mean, no, I wouldn't mind."

"Here are some Euros," she said, handing me some bills. With my heart thumping, I opened the car door and walked into the store. It was crowded with Italians and a few tourists, and people were lined up at the cashier. I looked for the cooler that would have the water bottles, grabbed four, and stood in line. I looked so definitely American that people gave me curious glances and then continued their conversations.

Maybe I could do this without saying anything in Italian. I handed the cashier the bottles and he rang up the amount. He told me the cost, first in Italian and then in heavily-accented English. I gave him the Euros, and he gave me change. I counted it—it was short by five Euros. Great. Now I had no choice. Had he given me the wrong change on purpose, knowing that I wasn't Italian?

In Italian, I said, "*Scusi. Mancano cinque, signore*,"—I'm missing five, sir.

Startled, the cashier looked at me quizzically and looked at the bills in my hand. The people around me all stopped talking. No one expects an American to speak Italian, much less with the kind of southern Italian accent I had, which was—as we said in the U.S.—pretty "down home" for Italy. He gave me a crooked, shame-faced grin and handed me a five Euro bill from the drawer.

"*Grazie*," I mumbled, scooping up the bottles before fleeing to the safety of the car. I'd done it. It looked as if I could still communicate with no problem, but I wasn't sure if I was relieved or worried to know how thoroughly Italian I still might be.

My mouth was dry and after I'd handed Carrie and Nicole and Phil their waters, I uncapped mine and drank thirstily. Italian water tasted the same as U.S. water, but I knew now, after my little interaction in the AGIP, that water might be one of the only things that was the same in both countries.

We passed the exits for Napoli and then Pompeii, and I stared at the blue cone of Vesuvius, which had loomed over my life for so many years. I couldn't believe I was back. I watched from my window as the jumbled buildings and dusty pink and beige apartments and houses of Napoli faded into the distance.

Two hours later, we drove through Sorrento across the Amalfi peninsula to the Amalfi Coast road and began the terrifying drive that I remembered vaguely from previous trips to the coast. The sheer cliffs dropped into the bluest sea imaginable. Tiny villages clung to the steep mountainsides, making me wonder how it was they managed to hang on.

"Oh, my God, Dad!" Carrie shrieked, as we narrowly missed a giant tour bus barreling toward us on the impossibly narrow road, suspended above the ocean.

"Shhh, Carrie!" Nicole exclaimed. "Don't look down if you're afraid."

"Or don't look at all. Shut your eyes," Phil suggested, hunched over the steering wheel. I couldn't see his knuckles, but I was sure they were white. Between the crazy Italian drivers, the wack-job motorcyclists, and the millions of tour buses, this Amalfi Coast road, the Nastro Azzurro, was a terror. In some places—especially around corners and the infamous hairpin turns—there was room for only one vehicle at a time; we had to listen for horns beeping from the unseen oncoming traffic, or hope the roadside mirrors would catch sight of the vehicle before we ended up in a head-on collision. I sure hoped I wasn't going to die in Italy. If I did, I comforted myself that at least I wouldn't have to face Morgan or any of my new friends again. That was sick.

Looking out the window, though, at the little shops and restaurants and the signs for each little cliffside town, a feeling of familiarity began to tug at me. The boys hanging out on the street, looking over a *motorino*. A gaggle of girls whispering outside a store. The plump figure of a *nonna* all dressed in black, market basket over her arm, making her way gingerly across the cobblestone street. How much I had forgotten! No, I told myself. I couldn't let myself go all squishy and nostalgic.

We finally reached Positano—a collection of houses, apartments, hotels, and shops pasted on the cliffs overlooking the bay, framed by three ancient guard towers. Even I had to admit that it was a drop-dead gorgeous view.

"We're staying here?" Carrie asked, craning her neck to look out her window. "For six weeks? Is there anything to do?"

"Yes, we're staying here," Phil answered curtly, his customarily pleasant demeanor apparently eroded by the strain of driving the Amalfi Coast road. I couldn't blame him.

Carrie slumped down in her seat, drumming her fingers on the armrest.

"Nicole, do you have the address of the apartment and where we pick up the keys handy?" he asked.

"Yes, Phil, right here," Nicole answered, holding out some papers. "And here are the directions to get to a parking lot."

She handed those to me. Great. "It's going to be quite a walk from there to the apartment with our luggage, I'm afraid, according to this."

"Why can't we park at the apartment?" Carrie whined. "Do I have to carry my bag a long way?"

"That's the way Positano is, Carrie," Nicole said, patiently. "A lot of Positano is accessible only by foot."

"Only by foot?" Carrie asked, incredulously. "We have to *walk* everywhere?"

Phil added, "Carrie, you know that a lot of Italian towns and villages are built on hills, and steep, narrow streets are the norm. This isn't Hummer or Escalade country."

I thought Phil's comment was pretty funny, but Carrie didn't seem to think so, judging by her dramatic sigh and eye roll.

We wound our way down a narrow street, crowded with other cars and pedestrians and guys whizzing by on Vespas and *motorinos*, and I saw the sign we were looking for: *parcheggio*—parking. A guy was motioning us in with his hands, but I didn't see enough room for our car.

"Is this where we park?" Phil asked, rolling down his window.

"*Sì! Sì!*" the guy answered. "Keys," he added, holding out his hand.

"This is the place," I confirmed, checking the directions our landlord had provided.

We unloaded our bags from the trunk, bid farewell to the Volvo, Phil taking a claim ticket, and we looked around to see where we were supposed to find the restaurant where we would pick up the keys for the apartment. I studied the map Nicole had given me and tried to get my bearings.

There were plenty of other tourists around, judging from their clothing and the English and German I heard, but most everyone on the street was definitely Italian. Here I go, I thought, and swallowed hard.

"Where are the street signs?" Carrie asked. I pointed to a wall at the corner. *Via G Marconi*, the rectangular sign read.

"Oh, like everywhere else in Europe," she said, smugly.

Nicole and Phil smiled. "Yes, Carrie," Nicole said. "Like places you've been before."

"It's just like usual, then" Carrie said, brushing her hair out of her eyes and adjusting her backpack.

I wanted to say that the *real* Italy was nowhere like she'd been before, but there was time enough for her to find that out. I studied the directions our landlord had emailed Nicole; they looked easy enough to follow, as long as we could find the signs. Worst case, I could ask for directions.

Ten minutes later, after winding through narrow, crowded streets with our bags, we stood in front of the Café LoPresti, the restaurant where our landlord had left the keys for us. It was a typical Italian restaurant, with an arched doorway and outside tables shaded by red and green Cinzano umbrellas. A few dogs slept in the shade, under the tables where their owners were having lunch. I handed the papers back to Phil.

"Here," I said. "The people in the restaurant probably speak English."

He smiled a little tentatively, and we walked inside. The scents of olive oil and warm bread floated to meet us. About a dozen customers, mostly Italian, were eating at tables, talking loudly, and laughing. A really hot-looking young guy with dark, curly hair, wearing tan slacks and a long-sleeved white shirt rolled up to his elbows, walked toward us as we trundled our suitcases over the stone floor to the hostess desk. Carrie elbowed me and grinned.

"*Buon giorno*," he said with a confident smile. Then he continued in English, thankfully. "You must be the Cowans. *Benvenuti in Italia.*" He held out his hand and Phil shook it. "I am Giovanni LoPresti, and this is my family's *ristorante*. Signore Crudele is your landlord and our very good friend.

"This is my wife, Nicole, our daughter, Carrie, and our friend, Alessandra," Phil said. They shook hands.

"*Piacere*," Giovanni said, looking first into my eyes and then into Carrie's. I struggled to take an even breath. He went on, smoothly: "Let me find my father and he will give you the keys and instructions." Before he turned to go, he gave me—and then Carrie—a blindingly white smile.

Carrie blushed and I bit my lip to keep from laughing at her obvious reaction. Here we go, I thought. But he was really cute, no question. He must have been nineteen or twenty and way too old for Carrie, but not for me. What was I thinking? I scolded myself. The last thing I needed was another Italian entanglement.

Signor LoPresti emerged from the kitchen a few moments later, carrying a big envelope. He looked like a heavier, older version of Giovanni, and he, too, was dressed sharply in an open collared shirt and slacks. *La bella figura*, I reminded myself. Italians really did like to look nice and appearance was very important.

Introductions made, instructions, directions, and keys changed hands. I tried to pay attention to what Signor LoPresti was saying, but luckily everything seemed pretty straightforward. From the corner of my eye, I tried to catch another glimpse of Mr. Italian Hottie, but he must have been in the back somewhere. After Phil and Nicole promised Signor LoPresti we would be back for dinner later, we left. Carrie kept turning to look back over her shoulder, and I whispered, "Too old for you," and grinned.

She pouted and tossed her head. "We'll see," she said.

The Italian sun assaulted us as we walked out of the restaurant. I blinked in the bright glare and saw Giovanni directing a big van next to the wall of the restaurant. It took up almost half the entire street, but passers-by didn't even seem to notice. They just walked around it, though some teenagers slapped its fender. On the van's side, I read *Parmalat*, in big green letters, which, I knew, was the brand name of all kinds of things like milk, ice cream, and gelato. Two guys hopped out of the cab and began unloading crates and carrying them into the restaurant. Giovanni laughed and joked with them and even took a crate himself after he waved at us, calling out, "*Arrivederci!*"

Two boys, about fourteen or so, had stopped to watch the unloading from astride their *motorinos*. I noticed Giovanni give them a piercing look, which they returned with surly expressions, before he shouldered the crate and walked back into the restaurant. One of the boys sneered at Giovanni's disappearing back, then punched a number into his cell phone, talking urgently, as he looked around at the passers-by. Then, saying something to the other boy, he jerked his head toward the street and they both took off, zooming around pedestrians and cars. What was that about? I wondered why these young guys found a grocery unloading scene so interesting, and why Giovanni was unhappy that they were there. Obviously, I didn't know everything about Italy. Had I become more American than I thought?

Perhaps they were petty thieves of some kind. Kid street criminals—*scugnizzi*? The usual pickpockets and purse-snatchers? Although, if they had been, Giovanni would have yelled at them to go away and probably chased them off, rather than just glaring at them. There had been an almost palpable tension in the air that crackled between Giovanni and the two young men. Was there something else going on? And if there was, what was it? Stop it, Alex, I scolded myself. Give the imagination a vacation.

"He seems like a nice, hard-working young man," Nicole observed.

"Hmm," Phil answered. "I thought he was a little too interested in the girls."

"Oh, Dad!" Carrie exclaimed. "You are such a dad, sometimes."

Nicole and I laughed. But my smile faded as we hiked

down the narrow, winding streets to find our apartment. I was back—I was really back. All around us, Italians laughed and gestured as they walked by us on the narrow sidewalks; *motorinos* and scooters whizzed past, drivers hollering to each other and at pedestrians. The familiar scents of Italy surrounded me—sweaty humanity, ancient buildings, the suddenly pungent fragrance of geraniums in window boxes, the acrid smell of benzina, and fresh bread wafting from bakeries. It was as if I'd never left.

Had I lost Alex already? I wondered. I had to hold on, hard.

Chapter Three

We found the apartment up a flight of narrow stairs leading from the street. The building was a faded pink with crumbling plaster. Above us, a balcony jutted out over the street with some potted flowers on it, and there were gauzy curtains at the windows. There was a downstairs apartment, number fourteen, and the stairs led us up to number fifteen. We lugged the bags up; Phil and Nicole caught their breaths, while Phil fumbled for the keys in his pocket. The door was an old wooden one with an iron doorknob.

"This is where we're staying?" Carrie asked, wrinkling her nose. "This is old and junky."

In spite of myself, I bristled and wanted to snap back a quick answer but stopped.

"This is a very nice place," Nicole said sternly. "We're paying plenty for it."

"Hmph," Carrie snorted. Just then, Phil got the key to work in the lock and opened the door.

I couldn't believe it. It was so much like my Italian friends' houses and apartments—the mismatched furniture, the small living area, the microscopic kitchen. I could just imagine the bathroom and bedrooms!

Carrie began exploring. "One bathroom?" she exclaimed in horror. "Only one? For all four of us?" She turned a stricken face to Nicole. "And where's Alessandra going to sleep?"

Uh-oh. Somehow, I had known that this was inevitable. Italian—actually, almost all European—apartments were much smaller than what we were used to in the U.S.

"You're sharing a room," Nicole said, after an awkward pause.

"I don't get my own room?" Carrie asked. Then she must have had an inkling of how she sounded, because she said, still grumpily, "Okay then, fine." She dropped down on her bag and sunk her chin in her hands.

"I apologize, Alessandra," Nicole began. "We—"

I smiled. "Don't worry," I said. "That's Italy. I know. It'll be fine. Carrie had better not snore though," I added, half-jokingly.

"I do not!" Carrie said indignantly.

Nicole opened up windows and Phil carried their bags to the room they would share. I took my bag to our room, and Carrie trudged behind me, mumbling. The room wasn't bad—it was small, but clean, with twin beds covered by flowered bedspreads, and a small dresser with a mirror above it. A chair sat in the corner and a wardrobe stood next to the dresser. The window looked out over the street below and at the opposite apartment house, whose window boxes were filled with red geraniums.

"Which bed do you want?" I asked Carrie. I probably could have pulled rank and taken first choice, but her parents were paying me, so I thought I'd be diplomatic.

She shrugged. "I don't care. Where's the air conditioner? I want to be cool. It's hot in here."

This time I just had to smile. "There's not much air conditioning in Italy in private homes," I said. "Electricity is way too expensive. Americans don't even think twice about how much they waste," I admitted.

Carrie's jaw dropped. "But we've always had air when we came to Europe."

"You probably stayed in hotels all the time," I said.

Carrie threw herself on the bed closest to the window, face down. "This is horrible," she said, her voice muffled by the bedspread. "I want to go home."

That makes two of us, I wanted to say, but decided it was best to say nothing at all. I unzipped my bag and opened the wardrobe to find ancient hangers. They would work. We unpacked our clothes, stuffed them into the miniature drawers, and hung things up in the wardrobe.

"Alessandra?" Nicole said, coming into our room. "I'd like to go to the grocery store and pick up some things for breakfast and lunch tomorrow. Would you mind coming with me? The refrigerator is tiny, so I imagine we'll be shopping most every day, just as I read in the guidebooks, and I'd like to have your help at least for the first few times."

"Jeez," Carrie complained. "I thought she was supposed to be my companion, not your translator."

"Carrie," Nicole said, in a warning tone.

"Fine!" Carrie groused. Then she brightened. "Can I come, too?"

Nicole stared at her daughter. "You want to go grocery shopping? With me?" she asked, incredulously.

I was pretty sure I knew the reason why Carrie wanted to go, and it was wearing pants, but I kept my mouth shut.

"We'll probably have to go to more than one store," I warned Nicole. "I doubt there's a supermarket in town."

"Of course," Nicole said. She pulled a list from her purse. "That's why our landlord, Mr. Crudele, wrote all these stores down. A-ha! Butcher, produce, bakery…we're set," she finished, cheerfully. Meanwhile, Carrie was brushing her hair and putting on lipstick, looking in the mirror.

"It will be good to be outside in the sunlight," Nicole said. "It'll help with our jet lag. Phil, be sure you sit next to a window so the sun can get to you too."

Phil was sitting at the square table in the dining area, his and Nicole's laptops up and running. "Yes, dear," he said. "We're in the wireless network," he exclaimed, with a grin.

"Can I check email?" Carrie asked. "My friends all said they'd email me, since I can't text or tweet or Instagram over here." She made a face. "It's like being in the middle ages."

I could check mine, too, but I guessed there wouldn't be anything from my American friends yet. I knew I should email Morgan so she wouldn't think I was a real loser, but I could always do that later. I'd email Mom and Dad that we had arrived safely, once we got back from shopping, and I'd email Caterina, Giuseppa, and Maria, too. With a sigh, I remembered how much fun we used to have, sharing secrets, giggling about guys, and complaining about schoolwork.

Morgan and the kids at Sonoma had no idea how rigorous an Italian school was; they complained about "all the work" at Sonoma High. Ha.

"Later," Phil said. "I've got to check in with the department and then with my contacts here. It looks like you're on your way out the door anyway."

Carrie frowned. "Whatever." She crossed the room to the front door and flung it open. "Let's get out of here," she said.

Phil frowned, but then he sighed and turned his attention to his laptop. Nicole and I followed Carrie out the door.

The grocery store was our first stop.

"*Buon giorno, signore*," I said automatically to the owner as we walked in. How many times had this simple greeting gotten me into trouble in the U.S., making my friends think I was terminally weird?—that is, until I realized that no one in the U.S. greeted shop owners and customers when they walked into a store, especially not people my age.

The shop owner smiled at me, raising his eyebrows. I already knew why. It wasn't only the Italian words of greeting; it was the accent. I was "down home," and he knew it.

"*Buon giorno, signorina*," he replied.

Carrie stared at me. "Do you know him?" she asked.

"No, why?" I answered.

"Then why did you talk to him?" she said, looking at all the bins of vegetables and fruits and strange labels and signs—Euros and kilos.

"In Italy, it's polite to greet everyone when you go into a

store, even if you don't know them. That's why some Italians think Americans are rude. We Americans usually don't do that," I explained.

"Hmph," Carrie said. "That *is* strange." She reached out to take an apple out of a bin and, without thinking, I grabbed her wrist. "Hey!" she exclaimed, her face furious. "What do you think you're doing?"

In consternation, I let go of her hand and pointed to a box of plastic gloves. I had done it again! I was morphing back into being Italian. "Sorry, Carrie. Put on a pair of gloves. It's not polite to touch the produce without them. The owner might get mad."

Nicole's eyes were wide. "I was wondering what those gloves were for," she said. "Alessandra, I'm so glad you're with us."

"This is so dumb," Carrie said, but she put on a pair of gloves and placed several apples in a basket.

We bought some veggies and fruits, and walked on narrow, cobblestoned streets to the butcher shop. Some young guys drove by on Vespas, and, seeing us, hit their brakes. The tires squealed, and one of them almost did a doughnut in the middle of the street. The passers-by didn't take any notice.

"*Ciao, bella!*" one exclaimed, brushing his hair off his forehead. The other two grinned at us.

"*Che cosa fai?*" one of the others said, wheeling his Vespa to block our path.

Nicole looked aghast and turned to me.

"Oh, my God!" Carrie said to me. "What are they saying?

They're so hot!"

Instinctively, I knew the phrase, *"Che schifo!"*—how disgusting—wasn't appropriate , so I used my Italian to tell him we were very busy and, in no uncertain terms, to leave us alone. Their jaws dropped in shock, and I grasped Carrie's shoulder and began to propel her around the boys and up the street; Nicole, staring over her shoulder, dragged Carrie by her other arm.

"Mom!" Carrie protested. "What's wrong?"

"Shush, Carrie!" Nicole said. "Remember what we told you about Italian men?"

"But they were just guys," Carrie said. "Oh, my God! You're going to totally keep me in jail!"

Nicole looked at me, mute appeal in her eyes. I took a deep breath. "Look, Carrie, you don't get it yet, but you will. A few Italian guys are just, well, pushy. Some of them will even try to grab your you-know-what if you're too close to them." I would have said, "grab your ass," but I was pretty sure Nicole wouldn't appreciate the graphic comment, although it might have shocked Carrie enough to make her pay attention.

Nicole cleared her throat as if to warn me not to say anything more, and Carrie said, "What? For real?"

"Uh-huh," I said. "Some of the ones you meet on the street, that is. Otherwise, if you meet boys through family or friends, that's fine. But you have to watch yourself on the street."

"When you were young, did that ever happen to you?" Carrie asked, curiously.

I smiled. "Carrie, when I was as 'young' as you, twelve, it happened to me." To her credit, Carrie turned red. That stopped her—for a while anyway. I still remembered how wary I had been of some of the guys in the halls when I first went to Sonoma High. Thinking they might pinch me or brush up against me or something, I'd gone out of my way to avoid them. It took my new friends, spotting another of my "Italian-Alert" episodes, to set me straight on that one.

"You're not really scared of guys?" Morgan had asked me, grinning, while everyone else laughed their heads off. That was another Italian quirk I'd discovered I had to leave behind me, thankfully! Living in Italy until I was almost seventeen had marked me in ways I was still trying to understand. I wanted so much to fit into life in the U.S., but I was definitely a work in progress.

Next, we hit the butcher shop. That was a whole other story.

"Is that really *horse*?" Carrie asked, pointing at a sign showing the silhouette of a horse next to a hunk of raw meat. "Grosser than gross!"

Behind me, I heard a smothered laugh and turned around to see a really good-looking guy, holding a basket. Were there *any* ugly guys in Positano? I wondered.

He was wearing a blue polo shirt, nice slacks, and deck shoes, and his dark hair fell across his forehead, but not so far that I missed his brown eyes. My breath left my body.

"The American *signorina* has a problem with our food?" he asked, raising an eyebrow. Of course, he spoke English to

43

me; we looked so American.

"Uh, no, not really," I said quickly. "She's just not used to it." I had a hard time putting a coherent sentence together as long as I was looking at him.

"And you?" he asked the obvious question. "You are used to it?" He sounded disbelieving.

"I used to live here," I replied.

"Really?" he answered. "An American? And now you are back."

"Oh, but just for a visit," I said, quickly. "Not permanently. I live in California now, in the U.S."

"I see," he said. His expression shut right down before he turned away. I must have said something wrong. Had I sounded like I was rejecting Italy? Had I violated some Italian-politeness rule that I didn't know about, or had already forgotten? Did he think I didn't want to be here? That was closer to the truth than I should have let him know. Italians are fiercely proud of their country, no matter its problems with Mafia and organized crime.

I held back a sigh. Either way, this guy was arrogant, and I definitely didn't appreciate that—no matter how good-looking he was. Besides, he made me feel different. And I wasn't even back in the U.S., feeling different. Here I was, now feeling different in Italy, where I used to feel at home.

Embarrassed by his curtness, I turned back to the butcher case and helped Nicole pick out several cuts of meat in kilos. She wasn't prepared for the procedure, and I had to dig deep in my memory for the amounts that used to come easily when I went shopping with Mom or Dad.

We finished at the bakery, but not before I ordered some *millefoglie*, the layered pastry cookie that had been my favorite. Two hours of shopping and we had enough for three days' worth of breakfasts and lunches. We lugged our bags up the narrow street, past the LoPrestis' restaurant, and, I have to admit, I did peer through the plate glass windows, wondering if I'd see Giovanni.

The two kids on the *motorinos* were nowhere to be seen, and I wondered again what they had been doing across from the restaurant the previous day. Dad would probably have been able to figure it out. Now, though, I was on my own. Apparently, besides not being able to fit in easily with everyone in the U.S., it now looked as if I couldn't fit in here in Italy either—if the snotty hottie's attitude in the butcher's shop was any clue. I frowned.

At eight that night, we got ready to go to dinner. I knew it was still too early to eat in Italy, but I decided to say nothing. I felt I'd done way too much of this interpreter-guide stuff for one day anyway. If I was going to stay "Alex" and move seamlessly back into Sonoma High School, I'd better back off and think American for a while. Carrie primped in front of the mirror, fluffing her hair and changing her outfit three times before we left. It was obvious what she was looking forward to at the restaurant, and it wasn't just pasta.

Outside, the fading twilight softened the buildings, and dozens of people crowded the streets on their way home. Conversation and laughter filled the air and brightly lit shops were filled with customers, tourists, and locals. We got to the restaurant to find that we were the first customers of the evening. It was empty.

"Are they closed?" Carrie asked, sounding extremely disappointed.

"No," Phil said. "People eat a lot later in Europe, remember? We'll probably do that, too, once we get acclimated."

Giovanni came out of the kitchen, smiling, and holding four menus. "*Buona sera*," he said, motioning us to a table.

"Ooof!" Not watching where she was going, Carrie almost ran right into the table. She'd been staring at Giovanni. He began to smile but cleared his throat and turned his head away for a moment instead.

"Tonight, our specials are linguine with clam sauce and *vitello*—veal *saltimbocca*," Giovanni said. "Would you like to start with a glass of wine?" Did his eyes linger on my face a little?

Blushing, Carrie opened the menu and studied it as if it held the secrets to everything she'd ever wanted to know. Poor kid, I thought, before I remembered what a brat she could be.

"Certainly," Phil said. Then he did something that endeared him to me forever. He looked at me. "Alessandra, would you like to join us in a glass, too?"

"Thanks. Yes, please," I answered.

"Hey! How about me?" Carrie protested.

"Now, Carrie, you know better," Phil said. Carrie slumped down in her chair. She was going to get permanent wrinkles from all those pouts, I thought.

I appreciated Phil offering me wine. He and Nicole had traveled all over the world, and obviously knew that other countries had no drinking age limit—particularly in Italy, where young people were expected to have a glass or two with meals. Twelve year olds were definitely included in this number, but Nicole and Phil apparently didn't want Carrie to have that leeway. Thank goodness! I thought. She didn't need liquid encouragement to be any more of a problem than she already was.

Giovanni and Phil consulted over the wine choices, while I glanced around the restaurant. Paintings of Positano hung on the walls, potted flowers graced each table, and the atmosphere was cozy and relaxing. I hoped the food would be good, which would mean we could come back. What was I thinking?

"*Ciao!*" a voice called from the doorway of the restaurant. A young man held a crate of what looked like wine bottles. "Giovanni! *Ecco il limoncello!*" He looked really familiar. Where had we seen him? He strode through the restaurant, carrying the box in front of him, and suddenly it clicked. It was the guy from the butcher's shop—the one with the cocky attitude who'd turned cold when I said I was American and didn't live in Italy anymore.

"Carlo! *Comé stai sta sera?*" Giovanni asked.

Carlo jerked his head toward the front door. "*C'è ancora,*" he said.

"Excuse me for a moment," Giovanni said to us. "We

have our limoncello delivery from the producer. I need to help carry it in."

Giovanni went out the front door, and I could hear loud conversations in Italian and thuds outside as boxes were being moved.

"What's limoncello?" Carrie asked. "Some kind of Jell-O?"

Nicole and Phil smiled at each other and then at Carrie. Of course, I knew what limoncello was, but I was done being interpreter-guide for the day.

"I'm just asking, you know," Carrie snapped. "You don't have to make fun of me."

Nicole sighed. "Limoncello is a very potent liqueur that is made in Italy."

"Southern Italy, really," Phil added. "Because of the lemons. They use only a few special kinds of lemons."

"And vodka," Nicole said. "Lots of vodka."

"Remember that night in Alba?" Phil asked her. Nicole blushed. I studied my menu. This conversation was going where I didn't want to go!

Giovanni came through the front door, trundling several cases of limoncello on a dolly. Now, I could read the boxes. *Bertolucci Limoncello, Positano, SA.*

Carlo strode through the kitchen door, past our table, and out the front door. He didn't greet us in the usual Italian way, but he knew we were Americans and didn't live in Italy. We weren't worth his time and attention, no doubt. Carlo then reappeared, rolling another dolly loaded with cases of limoncello. We could have been stains on the tablecloth for all the notice he gave us. Italian floated out through the open kitchen door. I could catch snatches of conversation, voices speaking about the delivery, it seemed.

Holding a tray with three wine glasses and a bottle of wine, Giovanni came toward us with a grin. Carlo followed him, rolling both dollies toward the front entrance.

"Carlo!" Giovanni called. Carlo turned, a mild irritation showing on his face. He must hate being interrupted while doing his job, I thought.

"Come and meet the American family staying at the Crudeles'," he said, gesturing toward us. Reluctantly, Carlo turned around and walked over to our table.

"Carlo's family, the Bertoluccis, are one of the biggest limoncello producers on the Amalfi Coast," Giovanni said proudly, clapping Carlo on the shoulder. Giovanni made introductions all round. Carrie sat up straighter.

"*Piacere*," Carlo said, with a perfunctory smile. "I am sorry, but I am in a rush to make these deliveries," he explained. "I hope you enjoy your stay." He inclined his head and left, rolling the dollies in front of him.

"He is a serious guy," Giovanni said, shrugging. "Always serious. But his family has a big business. He is studying at the University of Napoli to be an agronomist and take over the business. Liquor and wine production are big industries in Italy."

"Alessandra's father works at a winery in California, but they don't make limoncello," Nicole volunteered. "Have you heard of Nightingale Vintners? In Sonoma? It's a wonderful winery."

I froze. Great. Thanks, Nicole, I wanted to say. Bring up the winery—the very last subject I wanted to talk about. My mouth felt dry. Please, let's not ask any more questions or share any more information—just in case I might end up dead in the trunk of an Alfa Romeo. Well, if I were *lucky*, I'd be dead. I tried to reassure myself that Mom and Dad wouldn't have let me come, if they thought that imminent death was even a remote possibility. Of course, here in Italy, organized crime seemed so much more real—more real, at least, than it did back in sunny California.

Giovanni looked at me intently, as if for the first time. Then, he smiled, slowly. "A winery? No, I have not heard of Nightingale Vintners, but here in Italia, we don't hear much about California wines."

I couldn't tell if he was being snobby or if he was telling the truth, but I had the feeling that he looked down on California wines. Maybe now we could change the subject.

Nicole apparently didn't think he was being disrespectful because she continued, "Alessandra's father is a partner in the winery, and he and her mother speak fluent Italian."

"Really?" Giovanni raised his eyebrows, a double inflection that matched the disbelief in his voice. A fleeting expression crossed his face, but he quickly rearranged it before I could tell what he was thinking. Weird.

I felt my face get hot. To tell the truth, I didn't think all this information was necessary to spread all over Positano—and to people we didn't even really know. I couldn't tell if

Giovanni was truly interested or if he was just faking it to be polite. More importantly, I definitely knew any winery talk was off-limits. Mom and Dad's warning echoed in my head. Did my face suggest to Giovanni—or anyone—that I had anything to hide?

Phil beamed. "Alessandra grew up in Bari and Naples and she speaks great Italian too."

At this, Giovanni blinked in surprise and looked straight at me. "*Nevvero. Meraviglioso,*" he said. "*Benvenuta ancora, Alessandra!*"

"*Grazie,*" I said. "*Per favore, mi chiamo Alex.*" I might as well start off right—introducing myself as Alex. Giovanni tilted his head to the side, inquiringly. I quickly continued: "*Lei é molto gentile, ma il mio italiano non é buono,*"—you're very kind, but my Italian isn't good—wishing for this conversation to take another turn, and fast. Across the table, Carrie's face looked like a thundercloud. Phil and Nicole smiled encouragingly at me.

With a big grin, Giovanni unleashed a torrent of Italian, all of which I understood—about my accent, about whether I was happy to be back, and why I had moved back to the U.S. Almost against my will, a rush of warm nostalgia threatened to overwhelm me. Italian! My language!

"*Parliamo più tardi,*" I said, suggesting we talk later. I didn't like being the center of attention, and I especially didn't like being the center of Italian male attention. Alex, Alex, Alex, remember who you are, or who you are trying to be, I warned myself. I was American, American, American, and

I was going to fit in perfectly when I got back to the States.

"*Perché no?*" he said with a grin. *Why not?* Uh-oh. I hoped he didn't think I was hitting on him. I tucked into my dinner and hoped I hadn't crossed the line. With any luck, Giovanni was distracted from any winery talk, because I was *so* not eager to answer any questions about what it was that Dad did. Trying to answer those would push the limits of my creativity.

By now, other diners had arrived, and Signor LoPresti was waiting on them. The hum of conversation filled the air and dishes and pans clattered in the kitchen. We ordered our dinners and sipped our wine, while Nicole and Phil chatted about their books. Phil was working on a non-fiction book about the Saracen invasions of southern Italy and the Norman kingdoms, while Nicole was working on a book about the history of peasant arts and crafts in Italy.

Carrie watched Giovanni as he came in and out of the kitchen, waiting on customers and talking and laughing with them. I noticed that everyone seemed to know him and enjoy his company. Café LoPresti was definitely a popular restaurant with the locals, as well as tourists, which was a good sign. Although Mom and Dad had said that Italian organized crime had taken over some of the restaurants frequented by tourists in Italy, it didn't seem like that was going on at Café LoPresti. Everyone seemed to be having a great time, and I didn't see anyone who looked dangerous or sketchy in the restaurant. As if they would wear a sign, I thought. Still, I wondered about the *motorino* guys. They had definitely looked sketchy, but they had been outside the restaurant, not inside.

We finished dinner, with Carrie responding to her parents' attempts at bringing her into the conversation with a series of "uh-huhs." Gracious, she was not. Just as my parents had suggested, Phil and Nicole were very nice people, and if I was going to spend six weeks with another family, it might as well be this one. Phil was pretty relaxed, but I bet that he'd hold the line when he needed to. Nicole was more the "just let it flow," kind of person, but she was nice enough. Carrie, though, was a different deal.

After asking us if there was anything else he could bring us—"limoncello?" he inquired with a grin—Giovanni brought us the bill. Signor LoPresti visited with us briefly, welcoming us again and asking if there was anything further we needed in the apartment.

"What nice people," Nicole said, putting her glasses away in her purse.

"Alessandra's mother found us a nice situation," Phil agreed. Through friends of friends, Mom had found the apartment for the Cowans. See? I reminded myself. The LoPrestis were friends of friends of my parents. They couldn't be involved in organized crime.

Phil put his credit card on the bill as Giovanni appeared at our table. He smiled first at me and then at the Cowans. Carrie frowned.

"*Scusi*," Giovanni began. "Some of my friends from the town and from the university are coming here tomorrow evening *alle dieci*, at ten, to meet and visit. May Alessandra…

scusi"—here, he looked at me—"may Alex join us? It would be a nice time for her to meet other young people. She speaks Italian very well." He smiled at me and my heart skipped a beat. "My father and I will walk her home. Or you can come and fetch her at the appointed hour," he added, looking at Phil.

"Oh, *grazie mille*, but I'm not sure," I said quickly. Actually, I *was* sure; I was sure I wanted to get to know him better—as long as we didn't talk about wineries, but I *wasn't* sure that I should jump right in so quickly. "I'll probably be jet-lagged. I'm feeling pretty tired right now."

Nicole and Phil looked at each other. Nicole raised her eyebrows.

"It's up to you, Alessandra," Phil said, "but it sounds like a good opportunity. You'll be here for six weeks, after all. It might be nice to make some friends."

"But she's supposed to be with me!" Carrie complained. We all looked at her.

"Of course," Nicole said, soothingly. "She will be, most of the time. But you'll be in bed by ten."

Carrie's face turned bright red and she glared at her parents. Then she gave me a furious look.

Wonderful. Just what I needed. I could just imagine what these six weeks were going to be like.

Chapter Four

The night was balmy and beautiful, and people were making their *passeggiata*,—the promenade after dinner through the streets of the town—visiting with each other, laughing and talking.

"Giuseppe! Comé stai!"

"Ho veduto molte scarpe belle!"

"Dov'é la tua amica?"

The musical lilt of their Italian made me nostalgic for my old life in Italy. But, I reminded myself sternly, it was also that same life that had made it harder to blend in with everyone else back in Sonoma.

I was exhausted. As Nicole had suggested, our grocery shopping trip had been the right idea to try to adjust our biological clocks, but the strain of the last twenty-four hours was telling on me. I'd had to become accustomed to more than just a nine-hour time change.

Phil and Nicole had slowed down, too, and were no longer walking at their usual brisk pace. Actually, everyone in Italy moved slower, except when they were behind the wheel of a car or scooter. Carrie's lack of sleep only made her less-than-winning characteristics even more obvious, so I hoped we were going to go straight to bed.

We took turns taking showers in the miniature bathroom

shower stall.

"What are these?" Carrie yelled from the bathroom when it was her turn. "How can I dry myself off with this?"

Nicole smiled at me. "She must have found the towels," she said. Italian bath towels were about the size of face towels in the U.S., and thin—hardly the plush, fluffy ones we were used to.

"Good night, Carrie," I said politely, snuggling into my pillow as she came into our room, still huffing over the towels. Thank goodness Phil and Nicole had thought to bring plug converters for Carrie's hair dryer, or I would have been treated to another hour of complaining.

"Night," Carrie said curtly.

The moonlight cast a soft glow into our room. Outside, people were still enjoying the evening, and bursts of laughter and the lilt of musical Italian drifted up through our open window. Every sound I heard made me feel at home, a feeling I tried to push out of my mind.

"Can't they shut up already?" Carrie complained, burrowing her face into her pillow.

I sighed and closed my eyes. Tomorrow, we would explore Positano, and I'd meet Giovanni and his friends at Café LoPresti. I wasn't sure that hanging out with a lot of Italian students was a good idea, but it was probably too late to back out now without seeming really rude. I slipped into a deep sleep before I had a chance to think anything else.

"Time to get up, girls!" Nicole's voice called from the other side of the door. It seemed as if I had only just closed my eyes a few minutes ago.

"Nooooo!" Carrie exclaimed, pulling the covers over her head.

I looked at the alarm clock. Nine o'clock—back in the U.S. it was midnight, the day before.

We got dressed, Carrie in jeans and a t-shirt, and I in a skirt and a nice top. Nicole had probably told Carrie not to pack any of her short shorts, because they would definitely just serve as bait on an Italian street.

"*Caffè latte?*" Phil asked, grinning, holding up the Bialetti coffee maker—the "little man," as it was called. "I haven't used one of these in a long time, but Nicole got the right espresso coffee yesterday."

"What's that?" Carrie asked, staring at the little, funny pot.

"Sure! Thanks!" I said. What a great way to start my first Italian day, I thought. Then I stopped. How was I going to balance all this? Was I becoming Alessandra again?

We breakfasted on oranges and hard, crusty rolls and yogurt, sitting at the square table under the window, the Italian sunlight streaming in through the gauze curtains. Through the open window, we could hear the sounds of Positano waking up, people calling to each other, the cars braking and accelerating, and the high-pitched zoom of scooters.

"Is there any peanut butter for my roll?" Carrie asked.

"I forgot," Nicole said. "Sorry, Carrie. There was just so much else to think about. We'll get some today."

Uh-oh. "Um, I don't think you'll find any," I admitted. "Peanut butter isn't anyone's favorite in Italy, and I don't remember ever having any, except when we could get it from a military base. Unless things have really changed in the last few months, we probably can't buy it anywhere. There's always Nutella."

"You're kidding me!" Carrie exclaimed. "I don't believe it. What kind of a country is this, anyway?"

Biting my tongue, I let Nicole and Phil deal with this little problem.

"Carrie!" Phil spoke up first. "You would think you'd never been in a foreign country in your life. You've been all over the world and you should know by now that things are different everywhere."

"But no peanut butter?" Carrie wailed.

"You can live without peanut butter for six weeks, I'm sure," Nicole said. "There will be lots of other good foods for you to try. You can have a culinary adventure!"

"Like limoncello?" Carrie asked, mischievously.

"No, not like limoncello," Phil said quickly.

"I think she's overtired," Nicole said to Phil.

"Would you quit talking about me as if I wasn't here?" Carrie complained. But, I thought, her parents were right. She looked tired and acted even crabbier than normal. I suppressed a sigh. Was this what I had to look forward to today?

Nicole ignored Carrie's last comment. "Why don't you enter that little 'no peanut butter problem' in your journal?"

"You keep a journal?" I asked Carrie, trying not to sound like I was in total disbelief, which I was.

"Yeah," Carrie muttered. "My parents make me do one everywhere we go. They tell me I'll be glad when I get older—if I survive all the trips my parents make me take, that is." She slurped her *latte*.

"We got one for you too, Alessandra," Nicole said, smiling. She got up and went into her bedroom, returning with a bright blue book. "We didn't want you to feel left out, and we know you probably have a lot of thoughts to write about, now that you're back here. You could even write it in Italian," she added.

Not likely, I wanted to answer, but smiled instead. "That's very thoughtful of you," I said. "Thanks so much for thinking of me." I took the journal and riffled the pages. The new paper smell did make me want to write in it. A sudden thought struck me. What if I wrote in my journal—but as an American would if she didn't know everything I knew and had no Italian memories? Would that help me keep my head on straight? Maybe this journal could be my answer to keeping my American identity and not sliding back into my Italian one, so I could fit right back into Sonoma. Genius!

"Carrie, will you do the breakfast dishes, please?" Nicole asked after we'd finished breakfast. "And, by the way—"

Carrie frowned. "I know, I know, there's no dishwasher," she grumbled. She sighed heavily and got up. I followed her to the tiny sink with some of the dishes. She washed and I dried the heavy china plates and put them away in the cupboard.

"Well," Phil announced, closing his laptop, "I think we

should get the lay of the land, so to speak, for our first few days here. Shall we check out the beaches and see what restaurants are around? We have the list from Signor Crudele. There is a limoncello factory and there are craft stores and—"

"Can I lie out on the beach?" Carrie interrupted. "You guys can go on without me." She had the guts to smile a sweet smile. I would no more have left her on the beach by herself on her first day in Italy than fed her to a tiger shark, although that didn't seem like such a bad idea either.

"I think there's plenty of time for that," Nicole said, quickly. "I'm sure Alessandra would be happy to go to the beach with you another day. We've got six weeks. It'll be nice to look at the town and see what there is around—sort of get our bearings before we start working on our books."

Carrie sighed and flounced into the bathroom. Nicole and Phil looked at me with identical expressions of helplessness.

Phil shrugged and smiled. "She's really a good kid," he said. "She's just a bit headstrong."

"If she becomes a problem, just let us know, and we'll take care of it," Nicole assured me. Oh, sure, I wanted to say. I could see how well they'd taken care of it so far! At least Phil had a prayer of getting some control if he needed to, since he seemed to be a little more observant, but I thought some of the fluff from her textiles had gotten into Nicole's brain.

Armed with a map and Signor Crudele's list, we locked up the apartment and began walking. Nicole put on her sunglasses and began reading the map, holding the list in her hand. "I checked all of Mr. Crudele's suggestions and circled their locations on the map," she said. "So, we can start here," she paused to show Phil what she had pinpointed, "and go all the way there."

"Looks like the limoncello factory is up on the other side of Positano," Phil noted, looking at the map over Nicole's shoulder. "It would be fun to tour that one of these days, if we could."

"We should ask Giovanni if Carlo's family gives tours," Carrie said, suddenly interested in the conversation.

Phil looked over the top of his sunglasses at his daughter. "And why, pray tell, would you be so very interested in touring a limoncello factory?" he asked with a lop-sided grin. "It wouldn't have anything to do with the fact that that young man is, in your vernacular, 'hot'?"

Carrie had the grace to blush. "Dad!" she protested, giving him a playful shove.

Four hours and a long lunch later, we trudged back up the street toward our apartment. My head was swimming from all the places we'd visited—craft shops manufacturing the Amalfi Coast pottery with the signature lemon designs, gift shops where everything had a lemon motif, and clothing boutiques with floaty summer dresses. We trekked to the main beach of La Spiaggia Grande, and from there on to Le Tre Sorrelle, the restaurant of the three sisters, where we had appetizers. Then, finally, we finished off at Chez Black, where we had a seaside lunch next to La Spiaggia Grande. Everything was pretty much a blur.

"Nap time," Nicole announced, as we struggled up the

steps to the apartment.

"Maybe I'll go down to the beach," Carrie said. She held out an arm and examined it. "I'm starting to get white. I could use a tan."

At La Spiaggia Grande, I noted the number of Italian guys hovering around the female tourists stretched out on beach towels on the flat, gray sand. Carrie would last about fifteen minutes, I guessed.

"You should take a nap too, young lady," Phil said, in a tone that suggested he'd also made note of the loitering Italian guys at La Spiaggia. I gave him a grateful glance, and he winked conspiratorially at me.

"I'll take you to the beach tomorrow, Carrie," I promised. "I'm sure your parents have work to do tomorrow, and you and I can give them a break."

Carrie made a face. "Okay, fine," she said theatrically, and stomped into our bedroom.

Nicole locked the front door behind us and smiled at me. "Thanks," she said.

"It's nice to know we can trust you with our daughter," Phil said. "There were some real characters out there today."

"Well, thank you," I said quickly. "I'll do my best, for sure."

In our room, I lay down and tried to relax. Carrie was already asleep. I was getting nervous about tonight and Giovanni's little party at the restaurant. Would my Italian stand up to the stress and strain of conversation without English? Who else would be there? I was sure to be the only American, I guessed. It was too late for me to back out now, so I would just have to go. I asked Phil to pick me up at midnight, figuring two hours of Italian immersion would probably be enough.

I drifted off to sleep for an hour or so, but woke to the sound of loud honking in the street below. Carrie was already at the window, staring down at the street. I could hear people yelling in Italian, and the honking got crazier.

"Look, Alessandra!" Carrie said, loudly. "Come here! You need to see this!"

After groggily sliding from bed, I joined her at the window. In the street below, a young man on a Vespa was yelling at a guy who stood in front of a Fiat Topolino, a little "mouse car." The Vespa rider, it seemed, had tried to pass the Fiat in the tiny street, but the driver had cut him off. The two men gestured furiously, howling curses. A little crowd of curious onlookers had gathered around them.

"What happened?" Carrie asked. "Can you understand what they're saying?"

"Um, well, think of what the guys were saying in the last really gross movie you saw, and that'll pretty much cover it," I said, not wanting to translate Italian gutter language into English for Phil and Nicole's oh-so-not-impressionable young daughter.

"What did they do?" Carrie asked, leaning over the windowsill.

I pulled her back in. "You do not want to be leaning out of windows," I warned her. "You never know who is watching down there and will want to come and meet you. Wouldn't

Phil and Nicole love that?"

Carrie's mouth opened. "Come on! Someone off the street would come up here?"

"They might just hang around outside till you came down," I said, with a sigh. "If you were ugly, I wouldn't worry so much, but you're not." Maybe that little bit of flattery would help soften my warning.

"Oh, my God!" Carrie exclaimed. "Are you making this stuff up?"

"No, I'm not," I said, quickly drawing the gauzy curtains across the window. "Now, why don't you write in your journal? I think I'll start mine."

Opening my journal to the first page, I grabbed a pen and pretended to be deep in thought. Actually, I was still thinking about something the guy on the Vespa had yelled to the Fiat driver—something about how 'The System' would take care of the Fiat guy, that he would be sorry. What system? The *carabinieri*? The *polizia*, or—I swallowed hard—the Camorra?

When Vespa guy had mentioned The System, the Fiat driver had suddenly looked scared; he'd jumped back in his car, revved it up, and careened down the street. Even the rowdy little crowd gathered around had fallen silent. Whatever The System was, it seemed to have serious power. I could ask Giovanni about it later, but I felt—with a growing dread in my bones—that I already knew. The fact that all this had happened right below my window didn't make me too happy.

The System. I wrote in my journal. *What is it?*

I didn't dare write about what Dad was doing, but I wondered if this System might have anything to do with organized crime taking over wineries. If it did, I could let Dad know. Maybe, once I had told Dad all about it, my parents would yank me back across the Atlantic and I could still make Tahoe! I clicked the pen up and down with my thumb and then continued writing…

Ugh! I'm nervous about tonight, but I can just think about how it'll all be over at midnight. Will Giovanni spend time with me? Or does he have a girlfriend? Of course, in Italy, it doesn't much matter—the guys are such flirts, anyway. They're much bigger flirts than most American guys. But they're definitely hot. I smiled and tapped my pen on the page and then continued. *Today, we toured Positano, but I'm not sure how much Carrie really looked at anything except the guys.*

After a few more paragraphs, I felt more grounded and much more American. This journal could work out all right after all. I lay back on the bed and, closing my eyes, drifted off to sleep.

I woke up to the sounds of arguing in the next room.

"I have to email my friends!" Carrie protested. "Come on! I can't text anyone, you know."

"You've already sent at least a dozen," Phil said. "It's time to stop. Why don't you write in your journal or read one of the guidebooks? You're in Italy now, not the U.S., so make the most of where you are."

I rubbed the sleep out of my eyes and walked into the living room. Maybe I could help Phil and Nicole and get my emailing done too.

"Hey," I said, "Carrie, if you're done, can I check my email?" I smiled innocently.

Carrie's lip formed its familiar pout. "Fine!" she snapped. She tossed her head and stormed past me into our room, slamming the door behind her.

Phil shrugged and Nicole managed a queasy smile. "Teenagers," Phil said wryly, obviously forgetting that I was one and Carrie was not.

"All right if I look?" I asked.

"Sure," Nicole said, motioning me to the chair. "You emailed your parents yesterday that you'd arrived, right?"

"Uh-huh," I said. I checked my email while Phil and Nicole pored through guidebooks on the couch. One email was from Mom and Dad, asking me all sorts of questions. Answering those would take a while. Dad signed off with: "No worries. You're safe. Just keep quiet and have fun." Was he having second thoughts about my being safe? I spent some time answering their questions about what we were doing, how the apartment was, and generally reassuring them that everything was fine. Well, it *was* fine, except for missing out on Tahoe and my friends.

My friends… I frowned at the screen. Emailing Morgan was something I knew I should do, but I couldn't, just yet. What I wrote had to be exactly right, and I needed more time to think about what I would say. After all, I'd disappointed her when I dropped out of the Tahoe trip and made a mess of her carefully-made plans for the horseback riding. With a sigh, I emailed Caterina, Maria, and Giuseppa, telling them what I was doing and how I wished we could get together. Then, I wondered if my Italian friends would think that I was different too, now that I'd lived in the U.S.? What if I didn't fit in with them either now? I closed my email and looked at my watch.

"Yes," Phil said, as he caught my glance. "It's about time to get ready for dinner. We'll eat at the Café Positano tonight, and we'll take you to Café LoPresti afterwards. How does that sound?"

"Great," I answered, glancing at the still-closed door to my room.

"Just go on in," Nicole suggested. "It's your room, too."

"Thanks," I said. I knocked before opening the door. Carrie was curling her hair in front of the small mirror. She'd put on makeup and was obviously getting ready for a night out on the town, but the only place she was going was Café Positano with her parents.

"Who do you think will be at the party?" Carrie asked, looking at my reflection in the mirror.

"I don't know," I answered. "Giovanni said friends of his from the university and from Positano, I guess."

"How about Carlo, the limoncello guy?" Carrie asked, turning to face me. She never quit, I thought.

"Probably. Why?" I countered.

Carrie's face reddened. "Well, I was thinking you could ask him to take us on a tour of his factory," she said.

"Since when are you interested in limoncello production?" I asked with a grin.

Carrie set the curling iron down on a tile on the dresser. "I just thought it would be fun," she said, not meeting my eyes.

I didn't have the heart to follow up with a tease, so I just answered, "Uh-huh," in a noncommittal tone and began to change into another outfit.

"So, you'll ask him, right?" she persisted.

"If he's there, I'll try to remember," I promised halfheartedly, brushing my hair.

"Maybe I can come, too?" Carrie said, looking into the mirror next to me.

Great. What did I say now?

"Well, maybe another time, if there's another party," I said, thinking quickly. "Giovanni didn't include you this time, I'm afraid."

Carrie's face darkened. "You ask him," she said. "And ask the limoncello guy for a tour too."

Just what I wanted to do—ask for a factory tour from a guy who'd completely ignored us. With any luck, Carlo wouldn't be at the party tonight, so I wouldn't be able to ask him.

We had a delicious dinner at the Café Positano, after walking up the narrow streets to find the restaurant, which was perched on the cliffside, overlooking the bay—as were so many places in Positano. After dinner, we wandered slowly through the soft Italian night toward Café LoPresti and Giovanni's party, and my heart began to thud, jarring against the lilting cadences of Italian that swirled around us through the air. What was I getting myself into? I must be *pazza*—oops, crazy, I told myself, a little annoyed that I'd lapsed into thinking in Italian.

I was American, I reminded myself, and I wasn't going to forget it. I sincerely hoped Carlo was not going to be at the party, because not only did I not want to beg him for a tour, which I was quite sure was impolite and pushy, but also because he'd been cold to me twice.

Music, loud conversation, and the tinkling of glasses and china met our ears as we arrived at the door of the LoPrestis' restaurant. I could see several groups of young Italians laughing and Giovanni at the center talking with a beautiful, tall girl. I swallowed hard. Maybe I should just say I didn't feel well?

"I'll come and get you at midnight," Phil said. "Will that give you enough time?"

"Enough time for what?" Carrie snapped.

"Enough already," Phil said curtly.

"Sure," I answered. "Thanks." Taking a deep breath, I walked into the restaurant.

I was on my own, alone, and back in Italy.

Chapter Five

"Ciao, Alex," Giovanni called across the room as he spotted me walking toward him.

"Hi," I said. Instead of echoing his "ciao," I had decided that I would stay American as long as I could.

A flurry of Italian introductions later, I realized that there was no way I was going to be speaking English at all, unless someone wanted to practice, which no one did. It was scary how quickly my brain had already adjusted to Italian, which was a good thing, since my head swam with names and details of everyone's various university studies. They all seemed really friendly, though; many made comments about my "wonderful" Italian accent, which made me feel good. My vocabulary wasn't too up with some of the latest slang, but Giovanni's friends were really nice and laughed about it.

Guys flirted with girls, and vice versa—it was a typical group of young people, just like back in the U.S. One of the girls, Valentina, who was wearing a red top and had her dark hair pulled back in a ponytail, wasn't as friendly as the others. After greeting me coldly, she tried to cuddle up to Giovanni and proceeded to pointedly ignore me, even while I was having a conversation with Giovanni. It wasn't too hard to figure out why she wasn't so thrilled to meet me.

I was talking with a red-headed guy, Nicola, from Milano,

when, from the corner of my eye, I saw Carlo walk in the door and scan the room. His eyes rested on me momentarily, and his mouth tightened a bit. Wonderful, I thought. What had I done now? He looked really great, of course, with his broad shoulders, and his shirt with the cuffs rolled up, , but the look he gave me was positively chilling.

Giovanni disentangled himself from Valentina and brought me a glass of wine. He looked into my eyes. What was it about warm brown eyes that got me every time?

"So, Alex. Why 'Alex' and not 'Alessandra'?"

He got right to the point. I sighed. "It's shorter," I lied.

"But, Alessandra is such a beautiful name," he said, his eyes crinkling with a smile. "And it is Italian, after all."

"I know," I said. I took a sip of the wine, hoping it would make me feel better about this conversation.

"You know," he went on, still looking deep into my eyes, "it would help you fit in better here with everyone. Besides," he added, "it suits you."

"Thank you," I mumbled. The wine wasn't helping. Fit in, I repeated silently. But where?

"There's Carlo," Giovanni said, raising his glass to him.

"Yes, I saw him come in," I said. Carlo's scowling face reminded me of something. "There was something I wanted to ask you about. I saw a little street accident today and someone threatened someone else about 'The System.' What is that?" I asked.

Giovanni's smile disappeared and he glanced around quickly. Then he shrugged and gestured with his free hand.

"Ah, The System," he said, smiling again. "It's only what we call the Camorra and their business arrangements, Here, on the Amalfi Coast, we have the Sacra Lista, who are sort of like the Camorra. They are also part of The System. You understand?"

"It's like the Camorra?" I blurted out. Was the Vespa rider that I had seen in the street that morning a member of the Camorra, or the Sacra Lista? They were *here* in Positano? A chill ran down my back, in spite of the warm room. Was this Sacra Lista going to force its way into my life here in Positano? But they couldn't possibly know what Dad was trying to do, nor would they ever know I was his daughter, I reassured myself.

"Well, of course I know about the Camorra and the Mafia," I said, quickly. "I lived here almost my whole life, remember? But, was the Vespa rider threatening to send The System, the Sacra Lista, after the other driver?"

Giovanni snorted. "It was just an empty threat. The Sacra Lista is more of a business organization. They don't kill people."

Remembering the way Mom and Dad had talked about the Mafia and the Camorra, I had my doubts. If the Sacra Lista was anything like the Camorra, killing people was *exactly* what they did. Besides, if Sacra Lista was only a business organization, why would the Vespa rider threaten the other man with it, and why would everyone go completely silent when he did? I had seen the fear on their faces.

"What do you mean, 'business organization,'?" I asked,

my nerves suddenly on hyper-alert. While I didn't want to pester Giovanni with more questions, I felt that I needed more information in case I ran into the Sacra Lista on the streets again.

Maybe I should let Dad know that the Sacra Lista was active in Positano, after all. If anyone in Positano discovered that Dad was trying to thwart organized crime, they wouldn't think twice about kidnapping me and forcing Dad to shut everything down. A chill ran through me. I'd read stories of kidnappings in the newspapers and seen them happen on the Italian news on TV. It was life here. It was real. And it could happen to me, if anyone found out about what Dad was doing.

"You know how it is here in Italy," Giovanni said, with a shrug. "Business is business and you find the way to make things happen. The bribes are a way of life. Everybody needs something and if you can help them get it, it is better for you."

I nodded my head slowly. Giovanni wasn't telling me anything that I didn't already know. Bribes and connections were an important part of doing business in Italy, but no one thought much about it. And it wasn't just Italy—the U.S. had its fair share of bribery and corruption, as did other countries in the world. Still, I needed to be careful. Life in Italy was not always what it seemed to be on the surface. The ugliness spilled out only when people were threatened or when wineries were forced to sell out to organized crime because their wine stores had been destroyed. Dad was trying to make sure that didn't happen to Ralf's winery and to other U.S. wineries, too. Surely those things didn't happen to ordinary people, right? My mouth suddenly felt dry. Was I ordinary enough?

"But does the Sacra Lista bribe people, then?" I pressed Giovanni, trying to sound only casually interested. "Like for what? How does it work?" I needed to know just how much danger I could be in.

Just then, I recognized Carlo's back, his broad shoulders and curly hair. He was chatting with one of the girls. Giovanni noticed him too.

"Carlo!" Giovanni said, reaching out and clapping Carlo on the back.

Carlo turned around, forcing a smile when he saw me standing next to Giovanni. "Well, look who's here," he said. "The American."

"She may be American, but she is a real *guagliona*," Giovanni said, using the slang term for Neapolitan girl, which I hoped was a compliment.

Carlo raised his eyebrows and gave a half-smile. I could hardly meet his gaze, it was so intense. "Really?" he said. "And why do you favor us Italians with your presence now, since you already left us once?"

Attitude! I thought. But now I thought understood. He must be one of those Italians who thought that leaving Italy was a betrayal, and that anyone who chose to do so was *pazzo*, crazy. If I was honest with myself, I could understand that feeling. I used to think the same way. Before I could think of the right thing to say, Giovanni saved me.

"Carlo," Giovanni exclaimed, elbowing his friend. "Enough!" Grinning, Giovanni glanced at me. "Carlo is what you call *si lascia prendere nell'ingranaggio*."

I had to translate the slang in my head—'he was caught in the machinery,' was what I came up with. Giovanni must have caught my bewildered expression, because he laughed and said, "He works too hard—he's caught in a grind." Giovanni wagged his finger at Carlo. "*No?*"

Carlo actually smiled a real smile now. I swallowed hard. Were there *any* ugly guys here? Any at all?

"I apologize to you, *signorina*, for my impoliteness." Carlo bowed his head momentarily, and when he looked back up at me, he grinned again, meeting my eyes with his dark ones. My face tingled and I hoped I wasn't blushing in front of everyone. "Giovanni thinks I work too hard," he said. "He is always telling me to ease up and not be so serious. But my family's business is important. It's my future," he added, "after I graduate the university."

"My family's business is important too," Giovanni answered, gesturing around the busy restaurant, "but I can still find time to play."

Carlo shook his head with a grin. "And talk with the girls, of course." They both laughed and I tried to smile at the guy talk.

Valentina appeared at Giovanni's elbow, whispering something in his ear. "Excuse me," Giovanni said, with a lopsided grin. "I must tend to the family business." He left

Carlo and me staring at each other in a little pool of silence.

"Tell me about your limoncello business," I said, after realizing I was going to have to be the one to initiate conversation.

"Why talk about work?" Carlo said. "That's all I'm supposed to be interested in, according to Giovanni, so let's talk about something else." He smiled, and his dark brown eyes crinkled at the corners. My heart jumped a little. "Your half-empty wine glass, for example." He reached out to take it from me and I shook my head.

"No, thanks," I said. "I'm fine for now. So, really, how long has your family been making limoncello?" Maybe a serious conversation would distract me from looking in his eyes. And I did enjoy having *real* conversations with guys—something I had missed in the U.S., for the most part.

"You are really interested?" Carlo asked, his expression softening. "You are not just making conversation?"

I nodded, realizing that I would be seriously interested in *anything* he wanted to talk about, as long as I could stare into those dark brown eyes while he talked.

"About fifty years ago," Carlo said, "my grandfather and grandmother began making limoncello in their kitchen, and business grew, so my parents built a factory here in Positano. The lemons we grow here on the Amalfi Coast, IGP lemons, are the best, like Feminiello St. Teresa and Sfusato Amalfitana. You can tell the difference if someone uses lousy Sicilian lemons." He grinned. I smiled back. How different this was from the butcher shop meeting. Maybe he just wanted to talk to someone who was truly interested in what he cared about. "Now, of course, everything is controlled and regulated by the state, so we are in a factory with surprise inspectors and so on."

"Surprise inspectors?" I asked. "That sounds like restaurants in the U.S."

Carlo nodded his head. "They can close us if we don't have our workers wearing the bonnets and gloves and keep the machines clean. Also, they can close us if we are using the lemons that are not IGP, which hurts everyone's limoncello business. The limoncello will taste bad with the wrong lemons and will give all limoncello a bad name. You understand?" he asked, smiling into my eyes.

I nodded, trying to breathe evenly, though just being this close to Carlo made that almost impossible.

"And of course every limoncello house has its own secret recipe as well. But you must find all this boring," he said.

"No, not at all," I said quickly. Carlo's face lit up while he talked about his family business, which was very appealing. "It's like the winery my dad works at," I said impulsively. "Their grapes have to be of the same variety that they claim they are. They are also inspected. And there are special ways in which the grapes must be blended."

"Your father works in the wine business?" Carlo asked, raising an eyebrow. "He must know a lot about grapes."

Uh-oh. The wine business. I had been so taken by his eyes and in the excitement of our conversation, I'd forgotten my promise not to mention Dad's work.

"Well, he doesn't know much about wine really," I explained. "He's not a real vintner, but a marketer and translator for his friend who owns the winery." There was much, much more to it than that, of course, but there was no way Carlo—or anyone else, for that matter—was going to find that out from me. I could have kicked myself for bringing up the winery.

"I see," Carlo said. Then he smiled. "And now you are here, babysitting for friends, I hear."

News definitely traveled fast in Positano.

"Yes, babysitting," I answered. "I wish—" and then I caught myself. I had been going to complain about my missed Tahoe trip, and then realized how that would sound to him.

"You wish what?" Carlo asked, tilting his head to one side. My heart fluttered.

Stuck. Now I was stuck. Then, I had an inspiration. "Ummm, I wish you could give me and the Cowans a tour of your family's limoncello factory." Carlo looked puzzled for a moment, but I hurried on. "They've been wanting to see one, and Signor Crudele, our landlord, told us that your family's factory is one of the best."

"Ah, the tourists," he said. "Because of your Italian, I keep forgetting you are a tourist."

An American visiting during the holidays—that's exactly what I wanted to be, wasn't it? "Sure," I said, wondering why I was so annoyed about being labeled a 'tourist.' "If it's not too much trouble."

"No trouble," Carlo said, with a shrug. "You can come

anytime. We do not usually give the tours, but for you," he smiled at me, and my heart stopped, "of course. We are in production right now, so it's a good time. Just go to the front reception and tell them who you are."

"Thanks," I said. Now, Carrie would be off my back, for a while at least, and I might score a few points with Nicole and Phil. And I had the opportunity to spend more time with Carlo. He wasn't as prickly as I had first thought. As Giovanni had said, Carlo was immersed in his family's business. At Sonoma High, serious guys—with whom you could actually hold a conversation—were hard to find. I had drawn the line at joining the geek clubs, even though I preferred the thoughtful, intellectual type to the fun, jock guys in Morgan's group. The American guys were cute, but conversations often came to a sudden stop. Carlo, though, was different, very different, and very special. He obviously loved what he did, and that energy permeated his whole being. His smile and his enthusiastic conversation all demonstrated his deep commitment to a business that really mattered to him and his family. He was so different from anyone I'd met at Sonoma High.

Silence fell and for a moment we just stared at each other. I was so utterly mesmerized by his face that every conversational thought I had flew right out of my head. I desperately looked around for someone else to talk to, even though I could have easily spent the entire evening just gazing greedily into his warm brown eyes. To my surprise, Carlo grabbed my hand. His hand was strong and warm and my pulse fluttered a little.

"Come," Carlo said. "You're going to taste some of our limoncello." He pulled me through the crowded restaurant toward the bar, and I saw Valentina glance over at me through the crowd.

At Carlo's request, the bartender poured golden limoncello into two small, frosty glasses on the counter.

"*Basta!*" I said, gesturing to the bartender. "Enough!" I knew that a full glass of limoncello would send me flying, and I didn't need to be flying in this environment, particularly since Phil would arrive within a half hour to walk me home.

Carlo and the bartender grinned and exchanged a rapid volley of Italian that I could barely understand. I gathered enough to realize that the bartender was asking Carlo if he was chasing skirts again. I smiled weakly. Italian guys were Italian guys and they thought nothing of doing exactly that—skirt chasing and doing so in a very insistent manner, as if to say "you don't know what you're missing!" I knew I'd better watch myself, even though Carlo seemed like a good person. Giovanni, on the other hand, definitely seemed to be more of the typical flirt, and we hadn't had a meaningful conversation yet, despite our conversation about The System. So far, Giovanni had avoided any serious topics.

"*Cin-cin!*" Carlo said with a smile, raising his tiny glass. I did the same and we clinked our glasses together.

I took a sip of the potent lemony liqueur and could immediately feel it warming up my insides. It was deliciously addictive, tasting like syrupy lemonade with a huge punch.

One sip was going to be quite enough. I knew that I'd have to be very diplomatic about my refusal to drink any more. In Italy, politeness was everything and I did not want to mistakenly cause offense again! In the States, I had had to force myself to be *less* polite when we moved to Sonoma—it was kind of crazy! My friends would giggle at my formal greetings and salutations—to adults and teens alike. "Chill, Alex," they would say, after I'd politely said: 'How do you do? It's a pleasure to meet you.' "No one does that stuff here!"

Phil was expected any minute, and I was a little worried about his reaction if he should see me bellying up to the bar, drinking limoncello. Would he send me back to California? Could I still make it to Tahoe? That is, if Morgan or anyone still wanted me there. I winced, knowing that even after only six months in the U.S., I had already seen how changeable friendships could be, fueled by social media that seemed so much more important to kids in the U.S. than in Italy. I could already imagine Morgan's Instagram posts from this Tahoe trip: kids laughing, having a great time, and none of the posts would have me in them. Lots of people at Sonoma High would see them, too, and figure I was out of the group. Because I'd wrecked her plans, would Morgan decide my friendship wasn't worth the work of trying to turn me back into an American?

Giovanni elbowed his way between us and grinned at the glasses of limoncello in our hands. "Aha!" he said. "The Bertolucci family product!" Lifting up his empty wine glass, he looked through it and winked. "So, it is improving your

Italian?"

"This Italian," Carlo said, pointing to himself with his thumb, "needs no improvement."

Carlo was definitely not *my* Italian, but his reply was quick-witted, and I had to giggle.

"Really?" Giovanni retorted with a wry grin. "There is always room for improvement, especially in business. You should know that."

Carlo's face became suddenly serious. "No, in truth, *you* should know," he replied evenly. "You are always looking for the next big chance to improve things in your business." What was going on, here? I wondered, confused by the simmering air of antagonism that had suddenly materialized between these two young men.

Now it was Giovanni's turn to scowl. "Enough!" he said curtly. "You don't know what you're talking about. It's all just business. It's the way it is. You know that."

Carlo smiled and shrugged. "Business, business," he said. "I just stick to mine and you mind yours—*bada agli affari tuoi.* Okay?"

"Okay, okay," Giovanni said, smiling at me with another shrug. I had forgotten how many times Italians shrugged, and it made me want to smile. Shrugs were part of life in Italy, signaling a sort of easy-going acceptance. "I think Valentina needs some attention—I will let you two limoncello aficionados talk." He started to walk away and then turned back. "And it just may improve your Italian!" he added, grinning at me.

I felt irritated at Giovanni's comment that my Italian could be improved, but then I thought that I should be glad that people could tell I wasn't a *real* Italian because my Italian wasn't absolutely, absolutely perfect. Didn't I want to be completely, one hundred percent recognizable as an American?

Carlo sighed and drank another swallow of limoncello. "This is really good, if I do say so myself."

"Yes, it is," I said, taking another tiny sip. "What did Giovanni mean when he said it was all just business?"

Carlo glanced over at the bartender, but he was busy down at the end of the bar, talking to an older couple. "You have heard of the Camorra—The System?" he asked, bending his head closer to mine. I nodded, looking around the crowded room, trying not to seem too obvious or nervous, which I was. "The Amalfi Coast has its own version, the Sacra Lista," Carlo said.

"That was what Giovanni told me. He said it was just business and they didn't"—I paused and lowered my voice— "kill people. But, I saw a street accident today, and it seemed like more than just 'business' when the drivers were yelling at each other. One told the other that he would get The System after him."

Carlo frowned and twirled the glass of limoncello on the bar counter. "It was stupid of them to yell about it in the street. Part of it is business, yes, an ugly business. Giovanni likes to pretend that the other side doesn't exist— the extortion, the money laundering, the drug and women trafficking, and the small business owners who get forced out and lose everything. And then there is also the violence and the killing."

"Violence?" I squeaked. "Killing?" I suddenly felt cold, in spite of the warm restaurant. "What does the Sacra Lista do exactly?"

"Let's say you own a small restaurant or a store," Carlo said, leaning in to speak more quietly in my ear. "You need to buy from distributors—Parmigiano, pasta, gelato, olive oil, things like that. A distributor comes to you and says he can get these things at a discount for you, but you must buy only from him, not from any other distributors."

"And?" I asked. "What's wrong with that? You're getting a discount, right?" Wait a second, I told myself and stopped. This arrangement sounded exactly like what Dad had described between the Italian wineries and the distributors.

"It sounds all right on the surface," Carlo replied evenly, "but you have to realize that the reason the distributor can do this is that he has already cut a deal with the producers— the factory who makes the Parmigiano Reggiano, say—and he owns nearly all the trucks that the producers can use to ship their supplies. So, the producers are stuck, too—they have to use him as a distributor for the delivery, because otherwise they have no trucks and no way to get their goods to you. And, if you say *no* to this distributor, things will start to happen to you. Other restaurants using his discounted Parmigiano can charge customers less, but you are paying more, so you can't discount your prices. People stop coming to buy from you, and you lose business. You can go out of business."

"That sounds really wrong," I said.

"Also, sometimes," Carlo continued, "if you do not go along with it, the state inspectors can come suddenly and find rats in your kitchen or mice droppings in your storeroom."

He stopped and looked at me for a moment. Loud conversation swirled around us.

"You understand how the inspectors know exactly when to come, and how they know exactly what they will find?" He shrugged again, but his dark gaze was intent on mine. "You are shut down. Or you are beaten. Some stranger picks a fight with you, and suddenly you are in hospital with tubes sticking out of you. Or, one of your family members is kidnapped, and you won't get them back—or back in one piece, I should say—unless you give in to the Sacra Lista."

My palms began to sweat. Was I really hearing this?

Carlo continued, his voice low in the noisy room, "It happened to our family friends, the Albaneses, last year. It was horrible." His face clouded over and his mouth turned down. "This is how the Sacra Lista does business. As long as you play by their rules, you are okay. It's wrong, but it's the way it is. Sometimes, you can challenge them, but you need help."

"They sound very powerful—and dangerous," I said, shivering. "But they're not *here* in Positano?" Please say they are not, I begged silently.

Carlo took a sip of his limoncello before saying simply,

gravely, "They are here."

Quickly, I ran over Carlo's words in my head. Wasn't that what Dad was really doing? Challenging organized crime, no matter what the organization? Now, I prayed that this Sacra Lista didn't make its way to the U.S., or get involved with any of the wine distributors that Ralf used. The thought of Dad running into these criminals petrified me with fear.

But, what *really* scared me was the thought that one of these Sacra Lista guys here in Positano would find out about Dad's investigation—or even find out that I was a 'winery kid,' as my Sonoma friends called me. Who knew what ideas that might give them? I clenched my fists, then drew a deep breath. The Sacra Lista would stop at nothing to make sure they got what they wanted. And if what they wanted were California wineries, some innocent teenage girl could run the risk of playing right into their hands. That could be me, if I wasn't exceedingly careful.

"Alessandra!" Phil's voice called from the restaurant doorway. Startled, I quickly turned to shield the limoncello glass from his view; Carlo promptly poured the rest into his own glass. I gave him a grateful look and he grinned in return. Those eyes—that intense, warm look was going to keep me up at night, I could already tell.

"Everything all right, Alessandra?" Phil asked, threading his way through the crowd, giving Carlo a piercing glance. He was such a dad! I hid a smile.

I had to switch gears into English after two solid hours of Italian and it was a bit of a struggle. "Umm, yes, Phil. This is Carlo Bertolucci, remember? We met him here last night. His family owns Bertolucci Limoncello," I said. "Carlo, you remember Signor Cowan?"

Phil's shoulders relaxed. Cute. I'd have to email Mom and Dad and tell them what good care he and Nicole were taking of me. No wonder Mom and Dad didn't worry about my going to Italy for six weeks with the Cowans.

I frowned. The Camorra stuff didn't seem to have bothered Mom and Dad too much—any possible danger probably seemed a lot more distant and far away from across the Atlantic. The Camorra and the Mafia were simply "doing business the Italian way," in the old way that everyone accepted. Perhaps Mom and Dad also wanted to make sure I didn't forget my Italian. Did they think I was becoming too American and were afraid that I would reject the Italian culture I had grown up with? If they only knew the truth!

I swallowed hard. Knowing the Sacra Lista was active right here in Positano—maybe even involved in the restaurant!— was terrifying. No more winery discussions with Carlo, that was for sure—or with anybody else for that matter.

"Sure, sure," Phil said, heartily. "I remember Carlo." He extended his hand and Carlo shook it with a smile.

"Good evening, Signor Cowan," Carlo said. "Alessandra asks if you are able to take the tour of our factory, and it will please us for you to come. Any time is good."

Phil smiled. "That's just great! We'll do it. Thank you very much. *Molte grazie*," he added, in an earnest attempt to be courteous.

"*Va bene*," Carlo said, his eyes twinkling at me. "*Ci vediamo presto, Signorina.*"

"*Perché no*," I said. "Thank you very much. *Buona notte.*"

Before I knew what was happening, Carlo gave me the usual two kisses—one on either cheek and, feeling the brush of his lips on my skin, my knees went weak. We'd had a great time together and he had made me feel special, but now I worried that I was falling hard for "Mr. Serious."

I found Giovanni and thanked him for inviting me. Valentina was hanging on his arm and didn't look at all pleased to see me, but when she realized I was leaving, she pasted a smile on her face. As Giovanni gave me the two-kiss salute on my cheeks, I noticed Valentina's suddenly narrowed eyes. Made a friend there, I thought wryly.

"Well? How was it?" Phil asked, as we turned into the narrow street in front of the restaurant. There were still plenty of people out, walking and visiting, and the air was filled with the scent of rosemary, lemons, and gardenias. "Did you meet some nice young people? How did your Italian hold up?"

Nice young people. I tried not to giggle at his phrase. "Uh-huh, I did," I answered. "Most of them were older than me—at university. But there were a few who are still at a *liceo*…er, a kind of high school."

"And how was the Italian?" Phil asked, as we rounded the corner to climb up another street to our apartment. I could so tell he was a teacher, because he was firing off one question after another.

"It was fine," I answered. I thought briefly of Giovanni's comment about my Italian needing improvement, and again felt annoyed. Was I more unsettled by the fact that he thought my Italian needed work or the thought that I had actually wanted my Italian to be perfect? I wasn't sure.

And then, there was Carlo. My Italian hadn't bothered him at all. I didn't think anything about me bothered him actually, and I loved everything about him. With my fingers, I gently touched my cheek where he had kissed me.

We passed a grocer and the display of Parmigiano Reggiano and olive oil in the window reminded me of the stranglehold of distributors that Carlo had referred to. With a chill, I remembered the truck in front of the LoPrestis' restaurant the day we arrived, delivering produce from the Parmalat distributor, and the two boys on *motorinos*, watching. After what Carlo had told me, I suspected they were connected somehow to the Sacra Lista.

Was Giovanni in league with the Sacra Lista? Or was he just cooperating because he had been forced to? I remembered Carlo and Giovanni arguing about "business" at the restaurant and, with a shiver, realized that Giovanni knew that Dad worked at a winery and had, in fact, seemed very interested when Phil had first mentioned it at dinner. The more I thought about all of this—about Dad, Carlo, and Giovanni—the more nervous I got. I didn't need anyone making connections between my dad's work at the winery and organized crime. If they found out about Dad, what would the Sacra Lista do?

Chapter Six

The next morning, I woke around nine. Not a bad adjustment to Italian time, I congratulated myself, even if I had been out late the night before—well, late for a weekday evening in the U.S, not in Italy.

Carrie was still huddled under the bedsheet, her red hair straggled on the pillow. I got up, brushed my teeth, put on my robe, and wandered out to the living room to see who else was up. I also needed a coffee.

Phil was busily tapping away at his keyboard, and Nicole was in the tiny kitchen, hovering over the little coffee maker as it began to whistle. They both looked up and smiled.

"Well, it's Cinderella, back from the ball," Phil joked. "Hope no one thought you would turn into a pumpkin!" Lame, I thought, but he was trying. He definitely reminded me of Dad.

"Good morning, Alessandra," Nicole said. "Would you like some coffee?"

I poured some hot milk into the dark coffee in my mug. "Thanks," I said. "It was a fun evening. People were nice."

"I'm sure they were, considering how good your Italian is," Nicole enthused.

I reddened a little, remembering Giovanni's comment. "Not really," I said. "My accent is fine, but my slang needs a little work. Everyone was helpful though."

"Well, you'll get a chance to use it again, today," Nicole said, hopefully. "Phil and I have work to do, and we're hoping you'll take Carrie to the beach."

"She's dying to get out of here and away from us, I think," Phil added, chuckling ruefully.

"Sure," I said. What else could I possibly say? The thought of spending the whole day with Carrie on a beach with lustful Italian guys lurking after us was hardly my idea of a great time.

"We'll give you a key to the apartment, in case we're out when you come back, and some Euros for lunch; you two can grab a sandwich or something at one of those little cafés," Nicole said.

Panino, not sandwich, I caught myself thinking. Stop that!

"And be sure Carrie wears sunscreen," Nicole added. "Her fair skin tends to really burn."

"I'm sure Alessandra would have thought of that," Phil said. I smiled gratefully at him.

"Would have thought of what?" Carrie's voice called from the bedroom. Phil and Nicole exchanged glances. Carrie had seemed dead to the world just a minute before when I had left the bedroom. I could not help suspecting that she was trickier than I had given her credit for and that she had just pretended to be asleep so she could listen in on our conversation.

After coffee and a breakfast of hard-boiled eggs and yogurt, Carrie and I changed into bathing suits. I threw on a knee-length skirt and top, while Carrie began to pull on a pair of impossibly tiny shorts. How had her parents even let her pack them? Knowing Carrie as I did now, I concluded that she'd probably sneaked them in when Phil and Nicole weren't looking.

"Um, I don't think so," I cautioned. "Try something that covers you up more."

Carrie's face darkened. "Who are you to tell me what to wear?" she challenged. "My mother?"

"Look, Carrie," I said, trying to sound calm, "in Italy, short shorts are a definite way to attract the wrong kind of guys. You have no idea how annoying, and dangerous, that can be."

"Didn't you wear shorts in Italy when you lived here?" Carrie demanded, lifting her chin.

"Not on the street, I didn't," I answered. "And definitely not *that* short. And not when I was your age either."

In a huff, Carrie flung the shorts in a corner and yanked open one of the dresser drawers, rummaging through it to pull out a pair of cropped pants. She zipped them up with a vengeance and glared at me.

"There!" Carrie snapped. "Are you satisfied now that I'm dressed like a nun? This is *so* stupid. We're going to be showing a lot of bare skin on the beach, anyway."

"People expect it on the beach," I said, hoping that there wouldn't be any topless bathers at La Spiaggia Grande. How was I going to handle *that* with Carrie? No short shorts on the streets, but naked boobs were okay on the beach? "But on the street, some guys think it's an invitation."

"Italy!" Carrie muttered in disgust as she grabbed her backpack and stormed out of the room.

I understood how she felt. It *was* a little crazy, but it was just the way things were in Italy.

We took two bottles of water, two small beach towels, and our flip-flops, and, waving goodbye to Phil and Nicole, we were off. It wasn't hard to find La Spiaggia Grande again, since it was at the bottom of the town, and all of the descending streets eventually led to the beach. I hated to admit it, but being out on the streets in Positano was fun. The fresh, salty breeze met us at open turns, encouraging us to continue down through the town to the shimmering blue sea. Shops displayed their wares on small tables outside their doors. Blue and yellow dishes, decorated with lemons, were stacked alongside woven sandals; light summer dresses, embroidered with lemons and flowers, hung outside the shops and fluttered in the sea breeze. Lemons were everywhere, it seemed.

Tourists, dressed in brightly colored clothing and tennis shoes, lugged bags of purchases through the streets, stopping here and there as they looked in shop windows. Italians walked more purposefully in twos and threes, gesturing and talking. They dressed casually too, but a little dressier than the tourists; they looked more put-together. Exactly as I had remembered.

Tiny cars zoomed around us, *motorinos* whizzed past us, delivery vans rattled by, and guys yelled or whistled at us as we walked down the narrow street. I remembered to keep my bag on my inside shoulder, just in case, and made sure that Carrie's backpack was anchored firmly on her shoulders.

"Don't look when they whistle," I ordered Carrie, after the first two guys shouted, "*Ciao, bella!*"

Frowning, she muttered, "Fine," and scuffed her flip-flops on the cobbled street.

Every now and then, we came across an open gate and looked past the doors to see a courtyard with a fountain at the center, surrounded by pink and red flowers, or a table and chairs under a lemon tree. Above us, the golden dome of Santa Maria Assunta shone in the sunlight, and balconies, filled with flowers, looked like small gardens in the sky. At street corners, we'd catch another glimpse of the sea, before we turned and the buildings and narrow streets hid it from view again. I understood why artists liked to come to Positano to paint.

La Spiaggia, when we finally arrived, was hot and crowded with sunbathers. On the beach to the west, dozens of fishing and pleasure boats were lined up in rows, from the restaurant Chez Black to the tide line. People sprawled on lounges and blankets, sunning or reading or people-watching. Four guys kicked a soccer ball down by the water, yelling in some eastern European language. Everywhere, we heard Italian, English, French, and German.

"Where do you want to sit?" Carrie asked, scanning the beach.

I didn't want us anywhere near the soccer players, or

the two guys in Speedos—who had already noticed Carrie, judging from their gestures and stares. A raucous German family with three kids lolled in the sun, halfway between the restaurants and the water; they looked safe.

"There," I said, pointing to the family. Carrie looked a little disappointed, but trudged along next to me in the sand.

"Hey, Alessandra," she said in a loud whisper, jerking her head to the right. "Why do all these guys wear those little bathing suits? They're gross!"

I laughed. "I know—they are!" I looked over at Carrie, who was studiously looking at her feet. "Can you imagine guys wearing those back home?"

"No way!" Carrie said. "Yuck!"

"Really, Italians think it's gross how American men wear boxer trunks," I said, spreading out my towel. "They think everything's going to hang out all over the place."

Carrie began to giggle and, finding her laugh contagious, I joined in. Maybe things would be all right, after all. We settled ourselves on our towels, and I took out my book. Carrie had a magazine, which she opened and pretended to read while staring at everyone on the beach. I hoped nobody would be topless—naked boobs might just send Carrie screeching right over the edge. As a tourist in Italy, or in any country, it was always better not to call attention to yourself.

The blond parents of the family next to us slathered sunscreen on their three kids and chased them down to the water. I'd forgotten how many Germans vacationed in Italy—more, I now remembered, than almost any other nationality.

Drowsily, I turned the pages, getting sleepy in the warm sun. I laid my head on the sand and placed the open book over my eyes. Taking a deep breath, I inhaled the scent of paper and ink, my lifesaver and refuge when I had first arrived in Sonoma. My eyelids felt heavy and I thought a little nap might be just what I needed. The excitement of the previous night had left me more tired than I had realized.

"I'm going to sleep for a bit," I said to Carrie, hollowly, from under my book.

"'Kay," Carrie replied cheerfully.

When I woke, my mouth felt dry. The printed pages of my book had stuck to my face in the heat, and when I lifted the book off my face and rolled over, I was horrified to see that Carrie was gone—just a crumpled blanket lay on the sand. No Carrie. No backpack. No crop pants, t-shirt or flip-flops. Alarmed, I looked at my watch. I had slept for an hour and a half!

Damn! In an immediate state of near-panic, I sat up quickly, shaded my eyes from the glare and looked frantically toward the water. No red head bouncing around in the waves. Heart racing, I stood up and searched through the crowds on the beach from left to right. Had Carrie joined some group of kids? She couldn't speak a word of Italian—had she, by chance, found some English or American kids to hang out with?

The German family was coming back up the beach from the water, the kids giggling and shoving each other, and the dad trying to keep the kids from kicking sand on nearby sunbathers.

"You look for your friend?" the mother asked. She must have seen me looking all around.

"Yes," I said anxiously. "Did you see where she went?"

"She went over there," the dad volunteered, pointing to Le Tre Sorelle, the beachfront restaurant with gaudy red umbrellas.

"Thank you so much!" I exclaimed gratefully. Grabbing my bag, I shook the sand from the two towels, rolled them up under my arm, slid into my flip-flops, and walked rapidly toward Le Tre Sorelle. What on earth had Carrie been thinking? I wondered.

"*Che cosa fai, bella?*" one of the Speedo guys asked with a wide grin as I hurried past. While that kind of flirtation was absolutely the last thing I needed right now, I was relieved that both Speedo men were still on the beach and not off somewhere with Carrie.

People sat, lunching and talking, around a dozen outside tables at Le Tre Sorelle. A host met me at the entrance.

"Lunch for one?" he asked with a broad smile.

"No, thank you," I answered hastily. "*Cerco una ragazza con cappelli rossi.*" The surprise registered on his face—a tourist who spoke Italian as fluently as I did was unusual. "*L'ha vista?*"

"*Sì, trenti minuti fa. Non aveva abbastanza soldi per il pranzo. É andata la,*" he answered, pointing to the street leading up to the main part of town.

"*Grazie mille, signore*," I said, quickly, and began hurrying toward Via dei Mulini. Apparently, a red-headed American girl had been there half an hour ago and hadn't had any money for lunch. So why, I wondered, didn't she just wake me up to get Euros and we could have had lunch together? Instead, she'd headed into town and was on the loose —in Italy!—by herself.

It was only my third day on the job, and I'd already flunked out. My charge had vanished and I had no idea where she had gone. Panicked, I forced myself to slow down and notice everything. Think, Alex, think, I scolded myself. If I were a rebel, boy-crazy, hungry twelve-year-old, where would I go? There were guys everywhere, but lunch was another thing.

All of a sudden, it hit me—Café LoPresti! She would be able to not only wheedle some lunch, there, but she'd also have a chance to see Giovanni, without me. Carrie could have her guy, and her lunch, with no nanny to supervise. I sped up, anxious to locate Carrie once and for all, and then slowed as the thought occurred to me—if Giovanni really was involved with the Sacra Lista, the restaurant might not be safe. But what choice did I have?

I walked quickly up the hill, from one winding street to another, in the direction of the LoPrestis' restaurant. I scanned everyone along the way, just in case my theory was wrong and Carrie was window-shopping or chatting up some young Italians. Everywhere around me, people were involved in their own conversations and oblivious to my growing distress. I poked my head into shops, in case she'd stopped to look at a pair of sandals or try on a lemon-tinted dress. I asked the shop owners if they'd seen a red-headed American. They were all nice, their faces creased with concern, but nobody had seen Carrie. I asked them, if they saw her, to tell her to go home, and that Alex—no, Alessandra—was looking for her. I began to hope that she really had made it safely to Café LoPresti. At least there she would be with people we knew. I swallowed hard, wondering how well we really did know the LoPrestis after all?

Then, other, darker thoughts began flooding my brain...

What if some lustful middle-aged man had sweet-talked Carrie into trying on a dress because his wife was just the same size and he wanted to surprise her? Or what if some guys on Vespas had scooped her up and taken her to a party somewhere where they were all doing crack? Or what if she had been seized by Eastern European slave traffickers who drugged and blindfolded her before shipping her off to Turkey? Or what if the Sacra Lista had snagged her and would force her to sell drugs? Perhaps the Sacra Lista already knew that I was Carrie's nanny and they planned to use the kid against me and Dad and the winery! My imagination, fueled by books I'd read, was all fired up.

My mouth felt dry and I was already trying to figure out what I would say to the *carabinieri* when I reported her missing; I couldn't even begin to think what I would tell Nicole and Phil. My heart pounded with fear as I hurried up the cobblestone streets.

Chapter Seven

I had just turned away from the door of what must have been the tenth boutique I'd searched, when a voice called out: "Alessandra!"

I turned around to see Carlo. And next to him—with a scowl on her face—Carrie!

"Carrie!" I cried, a mixture of anger and relief bubbling up inside me. "Where have you been?"

"I just went to get something to eat," she said, defensively. "You were asleep and I was really hungry."

I looked at Carlo, who shook his head. "I found her walking up Via Vicolo Vito Savino," he said. "She was lost."

"I was not lost!" Carrie said furiously, glaring at Carlo. "I was just shopping on my way to Café LoPresti. I knew right where to go."

"Café LoPresti is not in that direction on the street," Carlo said. "You mistook yourself."

"'I mistook myself?' You mean, 'I made a mistake'?" Carrie retorted.

I blushed, and didn't know for whom I was more embarrassed—for Carrie's pettiness in criticizing Carlo's English when she herself knew no other language, or Carlo, for having his kindness repaid by a snippy little tweenager, or me, for being a fellow American of this horrible brat.

"Carlo," I managed to choke out, "I'm so sorry. Carrie is just a kid. She doesn't mean to be rude and we really appreciate what you've done." I shot a fierce look at Carrie. "You mean to thank Carlo for helping you, don't you?"

Carlo's face had frozen, for a moment, into the indifferent mask I'd first seen in the butcher shop. "*Va bene*, it's all right," he then said, casually. "I was calling on some of our sellers when I saw her coming in and out of shops. She looked lost. It's not safe to look lost and be a young American girl."

"Carlo," I said earnestly. "I'm so sorry! *Mi dispiace moltissimo!* I don't know what I can say to make this right."

To my relief, Carlo's face relaxed into a smile. "No problem," he said. "I understand." He looked over at Carrie, who was studying the pattern of the pavement under her flip-flops. "*Capisco tutto*," he said, with an intense, warm look that sent a jolt right through me.

He understood everything—the bratty kid, the language problem, and my embarrassment. I just hoped he didn't also understand that I thought him the hottest thing I'd ever seen!

"*Grazie tante*," I said, with a smile.

"I must get to work," Carlo said. "Maybe we will see you at Bertolucci Limoncello?"

My heart lifted. This little drama didn't mark the end of our friendship—or could this be more than friendship, after all? I smiled in relief.

"Of course, I would love that!" I looked at Carrie. "Hey, Carrie, you're going to thank Carlo, aren't you?"

"You're not my mother," Carrie muttered under her breath.

She needed a new line, I thought. "But thanks, Carlo," she said, grudgingly.

Carlo and I exchanged smiles. Did his eyes linger on mine a little longer than was really necessary? He raised his eyebrows and shrugged, still smiling. "I, too, have a little sister," he said. "*Tutte sono uguale.*" They are all the same— well, for his sake, I hoped his little sister was easier to deal with than Carrie.

"We'll be in touch, Carlo, and thank you again," I said. Then, to my surprise, Carlo firmly took hold of my shoulders with his warm, strong hands and gave me a kiss on each cheek. My face felt flushed—I was sure it had turned as red as the bag I carried. Then Carlo kissed Carrie's cheeks as she stood stock-still in confusion.

"*Ciao!*" he said cheerfully and, waving at us, walked into a nearby store.

"Now," I said sharply to Carrie, who was staring at me defiantly, "why didn't you just wake me up if you were hungry?"

"I didn't want to bother you," Carrie answered, looking away. She was a terrible liar.

"Carrie," I said, trying not to sound exasperated. "How many times do your parents and I have to tell you about making smart choices? This is a foreign country, and you don't speak the language. You look vulnerable and you're cute," I finished, hoping my last remark would soften her up. "You have to be careful. I mean it."

It seemed that I was getting through to her because Carrie

straightened her shoulders and had the grace to look slightly apologetic. "Okay, fine," she mumbled. "I'll be more careful." Then, glancing worriedly at my face, she asked, "You won't tell my parents, will you? They'll kill me."

I had been thinking about happily killing her myself at that moment. "Well, Carrie, they're going to have to know something," I said, carefully. "Carlo knows you were lost, and Positano is a small town. I can't just lie to your parents. We'll just say you went for a walk and couldn't find your way back to the beach."

"Will you tell them that I didn't tell you I was going?" Carrie pressed me.

I sighed and began walking back toward La Spiaggia Grande, motioning Carrie to come along. I wasn't going to lie to the Cowans. I wasn't comfortable with flat-out lying, and didn't do it well. There had been times when I'd really wanted to be able to lie convincingly, but had never been able to quite pull it off. That's just how I was.

But then, I thought guiltily, I wasn't really lying when I didn't talk about Italy with my new American friends, was I? I used to try to change the subject so people wouldn't get weird about my Italian life. It was more of an omission thing, wasn't it? After all, I had not told anyone—including Carlo— what my dad *really* did at Ralf's winery. I had to keep silent in order to keep everyone safe—that wasn't lying, was it?

"Look, Carrie," I finally told her, as we turned a corner, "just say that you were going on a short walk and didn't want to wake me up; say that you realize now that it was a very big

103

mistake and you won't ever do it again. Okay?"

"Thanks, Alessandra," Carrie said gratefully. She even smiled at me, which made me wonder if I'd done the right thing, after all. Smiles came too easily to Carrie when she thought she could get what she wanted. Nicole and Phil obviously couldn't manage her—what made me think that I could? Although, she did seem to be listening to me more carefully now. Maybe there was a tiny light at the end of this tunnel.

As my heart rate gradually began to return to normal, I decided we'd better have something to eat. I had no intention of going to Café LoPresti after what had just happened. There was no controlling Carrie, it seemed, and the possible Sacra Lista connection had me worried. I needed a rest from drama. I wondered again if I should find some way of letting my parents know about the Sacra Lista presence in Positano. Perhaps they would want me to come home immediately. Despite the headache of Carrie, I wasn't sure that I wanted to go back to California yet. Italy was beginning to feel more and more like home, and then there was Carlo. I sighed.

"Let's go back to Le Tre Sorelle for lunch," I suggested. "I'm hungry now, too."

"But I want to go to Café LoPresti," Carrie scowled.

"We'll go there for dinner again soon," I said. "For now, let's try something different. At Le Tre Sorelle we will have a great view of the water and everyone on the beach."

Carrie's face brightened. "Okay," she said, and we continued walking back toward the beach.

At every shop that I had stopped at to ask after Carrie, I poked my head in and thanked the owners, letting them know that I'd found her. Their faces lit up with pleasure and welcomed us back anytime to look through their products.

"What are you saying to them?" Carrie asked.

"I'm thanking them for looking out for you," I answered. "It's the polite thing to do in Italy." Or anywhere, I thought, but Carrie probably wouldn't get that. It was part and parcel of being raised in the Diplomatic Service, and in Italy. Growing up, I always had to think about being polite and courteous; hardly anyone I knew back in Sonoma seemed to think that way much of the time.

"I don't really understand why taking a little walk is such a problem," Carrie said. "There are plenty of people on the streets, and Italians are all so nice—as you yourself keep saying."

She really knew how to work something. I sighed. "Carrie, come on. You see enough movies and watch enough TV to know there are bad guys out there. Seriously, you don't really think you can't get into trouble in a foreign country, do you?"

"But it's Italy!" Carrie exclaimed. "Your old homeland, right?"

"It's not my old homeland," I protested, but even as I spoke the words, a strange feeling of sadness threatened to overwhelm me. Italy was a homeland of sorts though, wasn't it? Was it even possible to have more than one home? I wasn't sure what I thought anymore. Time for the journal and a good, strong dose of American-ness.

"Look," I went on, trying to collect myself, "the rule is: you don't go *anywhere* by yourself. It's not safe, and it's not a good idea to put yourself in sketchy situations. *Capito?*" I lapsed into Italian without even thinking.

Carrie grinned. "Gotcha," she crowed.

I flushed a little, but tightened my mouth and steered her through a crowd of German tourists wearing hiking boots, backpacks on their beefy shoulders. Yes—hiking boots in the middle of summer in Positano!

The host at Le Tre Sorelle was glad to see that I'd found Carrie. We exchanged an update in Italian, while Carrie and I ate our lunch at an outside table under a tiny umbrella. Carrie stared at the guys on the beach and checked out customers as they arrived at the restaurant; no doubt she wished for some cute American guys to talk to, or some Italian guys to flirt with.

While the waiter cleared our plates, I looked at my watch—three o'clock. I was completely exhausted after the afternoon's events. All I wanted was to get back to the apartment and climb into bed. The strain of trying to balance both "Alex" and "Alessandra" was already wearing me down and this was just my third day! Thirty-nine more to go before I could get back to the good ol' USA. The thought did make me pause, though—Italians were so much friendlier, generally, than Americans, and I felt as if some forgotten part of me were coming alive again. I sighed, paid the check, and we left.

"Come back to the apartment," I warned Carrie, as she began to head for the beach again. "I've had enough and," looking at her pink skin, I concluded, "you could probably do with a little shade."

"Come on, Alessandra," Carrie complained. "This is our first day at the beach in Italy!"

"And it won't be our last," I remarked. "Let's go, or I *will* make a big deal of today's escapade with your parents."

Carrie wheeled around to face me. "You would not!" she accused. "You wouldn't break your promise!"

"Look, Carrie," I said, guiding her through a crowd of school kids jogging to the beach, chattering in Italian, "a promise is good only as long as both people are honest. So you be honest, and I will keep my promise. You said you wouldn't do that again, but that also means you have to do what I say."

"What?" Carrie exploded, causing a couple of middle-aged women to turn around and look at us. "I do *not* have to do what you say!"

"Fine," I said. "Nicole and Phil will be really happy to hear how you took off by yourself today on purpose, without telling me, on purpose. Good thing they have me along to translate when we need to identify your body at the *carabinieri* station, the next time you do this and you're not so lucky."

Fuming now, Carrie stomped up the hill in silence. I'd won the battle, for the moment, but it looked as if my work had only just begun. As we climbed the streets, I thought of what Carlo had said about the Sacra Lista. If the Sacra Lista was really as violent as Carlo had said, then there was no such thing as "only business" at all—not even close, no matter what Giovanni pretended.

I swallowed hard. The corruption that Dad was trying to prevent in Ralf's winery was happening right here, with people we knew, and in a restaurant we liked. The Sacra Lista was here in Positano, alive, well, and thriving. I wondered if I should mention to Nicole and Phil the possible Sacra Lista connections at the LoPrestis' restaurant. But I couldn't say anything without revealing what Dad was *really* doing. And they might wonder why the heck I was so worried about some vaguely organized crime scheme that seemingly had nothing to do with Americans.

I couldn't believe that I actually knew guys, like Giovanni, who were probably involved in organized crime! I'd been worried about *Dad* putting himself in danger. Who would have guessed that *I* might be running straight into Italian organized crime myself?

As we passed Café LoPresti and turned the corner to our street, I thought of all our meetings with Giovanni and his family, and how nice and welcoming they all were. It seemed impossible that such friendly, respected people could be part of a criminal branch of the Camorra. I had read too many books, for sure.

We clomped up the stairs to our apartment and I knocked on the old, wooden door. Nobody answered, so I took the iron key from my bag, fit it into the lock, and opened the door.

A note from Nicole and Phil waited for us on the little dining room table. *We went for a walk. We'll be home around six. Let's go to Café LoPresti for dinner. Love, Mom and Dad.*

Chapter Eight

$\mathscr{I}$ was too tired to worry about whether or not we should be going to the LoPrestis' restaurant for dinner. Once back in the safe and familiar surroundings of our apartment, I managed to convince myself that my imagination was working overtime on this Sacra Lista business.

Carrie immediately booted up the computer.

"I'm going to take a shower and then a short nap," I told her.

"Uh-huh." Carrie didn't even look up. She was probably going to email her American friends and tell them about her nanny-Nazi, and her adventures in Italy with all the cute guys. I sighed, washed my face, and gratefully lay down on my bed.

I dreamed in Italian again. I was with Giovanni, driving in a car on the Nastro Azzurro, the terrifying Amalfi Coast road.

"Can't you stop?" I yelled at him, as he screeched around the corners.

"Alessandra! Alessandra!" a voice said insistently in my ear. Someone was shaking my shoulder.

I felt groggy and confused, as if I was coming up from the bottom of the sea. Opening my eyes, I saw Carrie's face hovering above mine.

"You were talking in your sleep!" Carrie exclaimed. "And

it's after seven o'clock, time for dinner. Aren't you hungry?"

"Dinner?" I mumbled, trying to orientate myself. I wasn't on the Amalfi Coast road. Giovanni was nowhere to be seen, and Carrie was still shaking my shoulder.

"What were you dreaming about anyway?" Carrie asked, sitting on her bed. "You were yelling up a storm."

I struggled to sit up, rubbing my eyes. "What was I yelling?" I asked.

"'Can't you stop?' and then a bunch of Italian words," Carrie said. Frowning, she looked back over her shoulder at the closed door and lowered her voice. "You weren't dreaming about how I—uh—went for a walk today by myself, were you? If my parents heard you, they might wonder what all that was about, and we had a deal, you know."

"No, Carrie," I shook my head. "I dreamed that I was on the Amalfi Coast road. Remember how scary that was?"

"Oh, yeah," Carrie said, eyes wide. "No wonder you were talking in your sleep. I hope *I* don't dream about it." Satisfied, she got up and began brushing her hair in front of the mirror.

I didn't want to tell her about Giovanni appearing in my dream. I cringed to think of the use she might make of *that* information. I also wondered whether my asking Giovanni to stop in the dream reflected my desire to ask him to stop cooperating with the Sacra Lista in real life. I definitely had to figure out what was really going on before I said anything to my parents or to Phil and Nicole—if I said anything at all. There was no sense in alarming anyone if there was nothing to be worried about.

There were two ways to look at this problem, after all, I reminded myself, opening the wardrobe to pick out an outfit. One, as Carlo pointed out, was to keep in mind that this was the way of doing business in Italy, whether I liked it or not. Two, was the simple fact that people were getting hurt, and perhaps I could do something to stop that. Still, the thought of hanging around with someone who was involved in organized crime gave me the shivers. If I accidentally answered one too many questions about wineries, someone could end up fishing *my* body out of the Gulf of Salerno. I tried to convinced myself that I was joking, with no success.

Showered and dressed, and after we had had a glass of wine on our little balcony overlooking the street, the four of us walked to Café LoPresti. Carrie stuck close by my side, as if she was afraid I was going to reveal something about her little excursion and she'd have to step on my foot to get me to shut up. I noticed, as we arrived at the restaurant, that there were no delivery trucks parked in the road tonight, but it was probably too late for produce deliveries. Perhaps the Sacra Lista would arrive with the trucks in the morning? Stop that, I told myself sternly.

Inside, Signor LoPresti greeted us with his usual genial smile and showed us to a table.

"Do you see Giovanni?" Carrie asked me in a loud whisper.

Nicole smiled at her. "No, I don't."

"Don't you think he's a little old for you?" Phil said, in his best dad voice.

Carrie rolled her eyes. "Dad!" she protested. "He's just

nice. Come on."

She was pretty convincing, I had to admit. Obviously, Phil and Nicole were persuaded, since they only smiled indulgently at their daughter and began reading their menus.

I, too, saw no sign of Giovanni. Maybe he had a meeting with the Sacra Lista I thought, wryly. At least he wasn't here to ask me about wineries. The less said about *that* topic, the better.

We ordered, and while we waited, Phil and Nicole chatted about their day. Carrie kept glancing around the restaurant, clearly hoping to catch a glimpse of Giovanni. It was another impossibly beautiful Italian night; through the windows, I could see the stars winking above the rooftops, and the melodic sounds of the Italian language floated all around us. How could a scene so warm and so inviting conceal something so sinister as the operations of the Sacra Lista?

The waiter brought our wine, poured it—I mentally thanked Phil again for including me—and we all smiled at each other as we clinked glasses.

"Carrie told us that you two had a nice time at the beach today," Nicole said. "She said she took a little walk while you were napping?"

Carrie looked warily at me over her orange drink.

"Uh-huh," I said, noncommittally.

"Carrie said she didn't want to wake you up to tell you she was going for a walk, but she knows now that was a mistake. Right, Carrie?" Phil said sternly. Carrie nodded sheepishly.

Amazing, I thought. Carrie had put just the right amount

of spin on everything and her parents were buying it, lock, stock, and barrel.

"Uh-huh," I said again, not trusting myself to expand any further. "The beach was nice, and we didn't get burned."

"Was it crowded?" Phil asked.

"Not too bad," I said. "There were a lot of tourists, mostly Germans." Who helped me try to find your darling daughter, I wanted to say.

"Carrie mentioned that you had lunch at Le Tre Sorelle," Nicole said. "Was the food good? Should we try it for dinner?"

"It was fine," I answered. "Sure."

"Speaking of trying stuff," Carrie said, hitching her chair closer to the table. "When are we going to go for a tour of the limoncello factory?"

Phil fiddled with his wine glass and Nicole sighed. To me, it seemed as if they knew perfectly well why Carrie wanted to go. I definitely didn't mind the idea of a tour either. It would be a good way to see Carlo again—but I'd have to find some way of letting him know to keep Carrie's little expedition into Positano a secret.

"Any special reason why you are so interested in the production of a liqueur that you can't even drink?" Phil asked with a teasing grin. "It wouldn't have anything to do with the son of the owners, would it?"

Carrie flushed. "Dad!" she exclaimed. "It's something to do, isn't it? And you all like limoncello, right?"

"We'll go in a day or two," Nicole promised. "Your dad has

some research he wants to do on some of the old Saracen guard towers, so we thought we'd take a picnic lunch out to one of the towers and enjoy the day tomorrow. You girls will like that."

Carrie's expression made it perfectly clear that she wouldn't like that at all, but she didn't say anything. Maybe she understood the close call she had had today in the streets of Positano and was finally ready to listen. Knowing Carrie, I was pretty sure her attention would be temporary, but maybe there was hope for her, after all.

Signor LoPresti arrived with a waiter in tow who served us our dinners. My nerves went on alert, and I tensed, preparing to deflect any winery comments or questions. Keep it light, I reminded myself. "Enjoy," he said in English. To me, Signor LoPresti said, "*Speriamo che ti piaccia; é veramente un piacere che sei ritornata qui*,"—we hope you like it; it's truly a pleasure that you have returned here to Italy.

Everyone smiled, and I said, "*Grazie mille, signore.*" But what no one else knew but me was that Signor LoPresti had used the familiar form of "you" to talk to me. Italians usually used the familiar form to talk to kids or good friends, but I knew I wasn't considered a child any more at seventeen; Signor LoPresti was letting me know that he felt I was truly a friend.

His gracious kindness also made me feel pretty guilty about thinking that he and his family were involved with the Sacra Lista.

But, after all, I didn't belong in Italy anymore, I reminded myself. I didn't have to feel guilty about anything or worry about not fitting in here. Sonoma was where I had to belong now. I'd better email Morgan soon, or she'd really think I'd fallen off the grid, and who knew how long it would take me to rebuild the friendships I'd begun at Sonoma?

We planned the next day's trip over dinner, and I resigned myself to a day with the entire family. I'd take a book and definitely my journal. For sure, I'd have to get back in touch with my American self—Alex. When I got back to Sonoma, I was going to have to act as if I'd never been back to Italy and that I hadn't picked up all my old Italian life habits. To help make that happen, I was determined not to get charmed by Italy—or Carlo; although, I had a sneaking suspicion that it was already too late, I admitted to myself, thinking about Carlo's magnetic gaze.

The next morning, Nicole and I went shopping for picnic lunch stuff. Carrie was stuck in front of the computer again, and Phil was engrossed in his notes and some books, reading, so it was only the two of us. It was nice not having to watch out for Carrie all the time on the streets. Hopefully, she'd get better about being guy-crazy but so far it wasn't looking too positive.

We got provolone—it made me crazy when people said "provoloan," instead of "provolonay," but that was my Italian-self interfering again—*salame*, Parma ham, and some other cheeses the grocer recommended. The crusty bread at the bakery was still warm from the oven and smelled delicious. On the way home, we snacked on a couple of rolls the baker had given us.

"People certainly are nice to you," Nicole commented, as we turned a corner and headed up the narrow street. "Italians are so friendly. I don't remember their being this friendly when we were in Rome a few years ago, so I am sure it's your Italian. That doesn't happen to me in France with my French, though. And Phil's Italian is strictly academic. He does all right, but it's mostly for research, reading, and so on."

"Uh-huh," I said, my mouth full of roll. I didn't want to get into a whole discussion with Nicole about my Italian-ness. I wondered if I hummed a little of the Star-Spangled Banner it would help me get my real self back—if I still knew who my real self was, that is.

Back at the apartment, we assembled lunch and put a bottle of wine and some plastic glasses in a backpack.

"Ready?" Phil asked, shouldering the backpack.

"Do I really have to go?" Carrie asked, still at the computer, her fingers flying over the keyboard.

"Of course, you do," Nicole answered. "The guard tower is so interesting; it's centuries old and your dad has lots of great stories he can tell us about the Saracen pirates invading Positano."

I was pretty sure this was not going to make Carrie anxious to come along, but she was their daughter and I wasn't going to get in the middle of it. I grabbed my journal, put it in my bag, and waited.

"What your mother isn't telling you is that you are coming

with us. This is a family vacation and you are not going to stay by yourself in the middle of Positano," Phil said, more sternly.

"Oh, my God!" Carrie exclaimed. "You don't trust me, do you?"

It was all I could do to choke back my laughter. What a shock! I wanted to say. Our adventure yesterday was certainly not the first time Carrie had done something crazy, and was probably the reason they had hired me; it was either me or an ankle monitor.

Carrie's grumbling done, the four of us trooped down the stairs and walked through the sunlit streets to the path that led to La Spiaggia del Fornillo and to Il Torre Clavel. As we walked on the wharf, we could see the hulking medieval guard tower at the bottom of the cliff in the distance.

"I saw that from the beach yesterday," Carrie exclaimed. "Oh my God, we are really going to walk out there?"

"Yes," Phil said. "We can't go in it. It's a private home and it's rented out for a pretty penny, I understand."

"I think I read it was about $70,000 a month for the whole place," Nicole said. "The Torre Clavel is named after the French artist who bought it and renovated it."

"I didn't think 'Clavel' sounded Italian," Carrie said, trying to sound important. Was she really trying to get into this Italian thing?

We climbed a set of stone steps from the wharf and began walking along the paved path toward La Spiaggia del Fornillo, the sea to our left, and a sheer cliff to our right.

"Look how ancient these are," Phil said, pointing to the steps and bridges cut into the rock cliff ahead. "The Normans, when they ruled this part of Italy, really knew how to build defenses right out of the rock."

"I forgot the Normans were here too," I said, looking down at the surf lapping against the base of the cliffs far below.

The beach of Il Fornillo opened up in front of us, with a few hotels and restaurants fronting the small sandy beach. People lay on beach towels and under umbrellas.

"The Normans were everywhere," Phil said. "They ruled this part of Italy for centuries."

"Did the Saracens invade Italy during the Norman period?" I asked. "You said these were towers to protect against the Saracens?" I remembered hearing about the Saracens, or the Moors as they were called, when we lived in Napoli—pirates from Africa.

"Carrie! Watch where you're going!" Nicole cautioned. As we crossed the beach, Carrie must have been distracted by some guys, because she almost walked right into someone's beach umbrella.

"Mom!" she protested. "I'm fine! Oh, my gosh, can't you leave me alone for one second? Don't you think I can see where I'm walking?"

"Your mother wouldn't have said anything if you hadn't almost walked right into that poor man's umbrella," Phil said calmly.

Carrie tossed her head and clomped on ahead in her flip-flops. The pathway was amazing; it threaded along the side of the cliff, formed by dozens of steps up and around sheer rock, with the guard tower standing majestically at the end. A low wall divided us from the drop to the sea below, and trees grew from planters, providing welcoming pools of shade. Tourists sat on stone benches cut into the cliff, or stood, taking pictures of the turquoise sea, the medieval guard tower, and the rock islands in the bay. Phil said the islands were named Li Galli, the little roosters.

Around a bend in the path, I saw two Italian men in slacks and rolled-up shirt sleeves, gesturing and talking at one of the benches. This route seemed to be dominated by tourists, so it seemed odd to see Italians here. There was something familiar about one of them. And then, when one of the men turned and pointed back toward Positano, I stopped in startled surprise. It was Carlo! What was he doing way out here? I wondered.

As we approached, Carrie exclaimed, "It's Carlo! Oh, my gosh, it's Carlo!" She looked at Nicole. "Let's say hi!"

The two men were clearly deep in conversation but I couldn't hear anything that passed between them, their quiet voices drowned out by the sound of the waves rolling in and crashing below us. Carlo's companion was much older—perhaps forty-five or fifty. What were they doing way out here in such an isolated spot?

"He looks busy, Carrie," Nicole warned her.

"Carlo!" Carrie cried out.

Immediately, Carlo turned around. For a second, I thought

his startled expression seemed a strange combination of anger and wariness, but then he smiled tightly. His friend looked quizzically at Carlo. Carlo glanced around quickly before approaching us, and his friend frowned, folded his arms, and stared at us as we approached.

"Ah, the Cowan family, my favorite tourists. And Alessandra," Carlo said. "Signora Cowan, Signor Cowan, Carrie, and Alessandra, this is my…uh…agronomy professor from the university, Professor Scioscia. He comes to talk with me about the lemon crops."

Prof. Scioscia smiled and said, "*Piacere.*" Maybe it *was* a pleasure to meet us, but his eyes certainly didn't look pleased, nor did Carlo look happy to have us interrupt their meeting.

We shook hands, and murmured, "Pleased to meet you," and a variety of other polite greetings.

An awkward silence fell, and Carlo cleared his throat.

I quickly said, "I'm sure you're busy. Nice to see you. *Piacere,*" and walked toward the rest area ahead. Fortunately, Phil and Nicole got the hint and propelled Carrie along with them.

I stood at the wall, looking out to Le Galli—definitely a photo-op with rocky crags jutting out of the azure sea, but I wasn't thinking about photography. Something about the way these two men had been talking just didn't seem right. What was Carlo doing with an agronomy professor way out here? Why hadn't they arranged to meet at the factory? Or in the lemon groves? I wasn't sure what agronomy professors dressed like in Italy—jeans and sweatshirts?—but this guy, with his nice haircut, slacks, and expensive-looking shoes, didn't seem to be what I imagined an agronomy professor would look like.

But if he wasn't a professor, what was he?

Chapter Nine

We settled on our picnic blanket and Nicole handed out lunch. I looked back to where Carlo and Prof. Scioscia—if that really was his name—had been standing. They were gone.

"Meeting about lemons, eh?" Phil asked, noticing my glance. He swirled his wine in his plastic glass, which seemed a funny, gourmet-ish thing to do, considering the glass was plastic. "I read that if you don't use the right lemons to make limoncello, the liqueur will be inferior. The type of lemons you must use is regulated by the government. The same kind of rules that wineries are also subject to," he said with a smile at me. "You would know about that. Lots of regulations in wineries too."

"Carlo told me they have inspectors who come to the factory to make sure they are using the kind of lemons they say they are," I volunteered. I wasn't too thrilled about discussing wineries, regulations, and grapes—even with the Cowans.

"So, can we visit the factory tomorrow?" Carrie asked, almost bouncing up and down on the stone bench.

Nicole and Phil grinned at each other. "Well," Phil said, "I guess we can go tomorrow. I need a little break from the Saracens anyway."

I wasn't sure that I was really excited to visit the Bertoluccis' factory now, since we'd interrupted Carlo in his meeting. There could be only one reason he chose to meet this guy away from his factory at a place where usually only tourists went—he wanted to keep the meeting secret. But why? Could Carlo possibly be involved with the Sacra Lista? My heart sank.

He was too nice, too straight, too real, I told myself—wasn't he? I was thinking about Carlo more than was good for me, especially after having known him for only a few days. There was just something about him; he seemed different from other guys I had met. Maybe it was his seriousness combined with his wry sense of humor or his obvious dedication to his work. All I knew was that I wanted to be around him all the time. Oh, and not to mention how hot he was!

"Well, Carlo said we could stop by anytime," I said. We might as well get it over with and then Carrie would stop bugging me. I knew her well enough now to know that when she had her mind set on something she would never let it go. And, I admitted to myself, I definitely didn't mind seeing Carlo again. When I stopped to think about it, I couldn't believe that Carlo could actually be involved with the Sacra Lista. My heart sank at the thought. I was sure there must be a good explanation of his secret meeting with his 'professor,' and I was determined to find out what it was.

"Great!" Carrie said, a grin spreading across her face.

For the next hour, Phil took notes on the Norman architectural surroundings, Nicole and I read, while Carrie thumbed through an Italian celebrity magazine and peered through the iron gates at Il Torre Clavel. No doubt she was hoping for a couple of hotties to come along, but everyone who passed by were either middle-aged adults or German teenagers.

My thoughts kept returning to Carlo, and I realized that I, too, was hiding things from him. Even if Carlo wasn't involved with the Sacra Lista, there was no way I was going to let Carlo know about Dad and the Camorra stuff.

I sighed and turned back to my book. What was wrong with me?

"Let's head back," Nicole said, looking at her watch. "I was going to try and cook tonight, so I need to do a little food shopping. Alessandra?" she said as looked at me. "Are you able to come along?"

"Me too?" Carrie asked.

"Such culinary interest," Phil kidded her.

"Well!" Carrie exclaimed. "Oh, my God! I didn't come to Italy to be a prisoner in an apartment!"

"Calm down," Phil said. "I was just teasing you."

We threaded our way across the crowded wharf and made our way back to the apartment. We passed the LoPrestis' restaurant and although I looked for a delivery van, I saw only the usual tourists and *motorino* traffic. I didn't really want to see Giovanni yet either, but Carrie noticeably slowed her pace as we passed the restaurant.

"Come on, Carrie," Nicole urged. "You don't need to be hanging around Italian men."

"Young lady," Phil said with a frown, "I hope you're minding your manners around here?"

"Dad!" Carrie exclaimed. "Seriously! You want to turn me into a nun or something!"

I guess neither Nicole nor Phil thought there was any appropriate answer to that, or maybe they'd heard it too many times, because they just kept walking and started a conversation about dinner.

The next morning, we had a leisurely breakfast on the balcony overlooking the street. Phil got out a map of Positano and herded us out the door.

"I'm taking my camera," Nicole said. "It'll be fun to show everyone pictures of a real limoncello factory."

"Mom!" Carrie protested. "That's so touristy!"

As if she didn't act like one herself, I wanted to say, but thought better of it.

"I'm sure Carlo won't mind our taking pictures," Phil said.

About *that*, I wasn't so sure. Limoncello production and recipes were closely guarded secrets, so there might not be any pictures allowed.

We picked up our car at the *parcheggio*, Carrie complaining all the way about the hike up to the parking lot.

"We could have taken a taxi or a shuttle," Phil said as he handed Euros to the parking lot attendant, "but it would have cost just as much, maybe more, and this way, we're not tied to a schedule."

Phil drove us up the narrow, winding streets to the Bertolucci factory on the outskirts of town. On the way, we saw a number of lemon groves shaded by tarps. We could see fat lemons hanging from the trees, between the rows of poles that were holding up the tarps.

"Why do they cover the trees with tarps?" Carrie asked, when we stopped to let a family cross the road, the dad wheeling a bicycle with a baby on the back.

"You can ask Carlo, if he's there," Nicole said.

"It'll give you a good excuse to talk to him," Phil said, grinning in the rearview mirror.

"Dad!" Carrie said, turning her head to look out the window again.

"This must be it," Phil said, pulling up in front of a plain-looking white building with a tile roof and an arched doorway framed by two lemon trees. The tires crunched on the gravel as we came to a stop next to the building.

Bertolucci Limoncello, SA, I read above the doorway. What would Carlo's reaction be to me today? Would he pretend as if nothing had happened yesterday at Il Torre Clavel? I followed Nicole and Phil inside, Carrie trailing behind. As soon as we walked in, Nicole and Phil stood aside, and Nicole motioned me to the front—naturally, in case no one spoke English. Inside, the fragrance of lemons filled the air.

A pretty young girl sat at a front table with a computer and a phone. Shelves of files were arranged on a wall behind her. Painted on the wall above the files were branches of lemon trees with fat globes of yellow fruit hanging from them.

"Yes," she greeted us in accented English, "may I help you?"

I cleared my throat, glad, for once, not to have to translate. "Carlo invited us to tour the factory," I explained. "These are the Cowans. I'm—I'm Alessandra," I managed to say, remembering the Cowans were determined to call me Alessandra, much as I hadn't liked it at the beginning of our trip. Now, it began to seem very familiar, almost comforting.

The girl's face lit up. "Of course!" She stood, extending her hand. "I'm Giulietta, Carlo's sister. You are welcome. I will call Carlo. He is here."

Giulietta spoke on the phone in rapid Italian, telling Carlo that the American tourist family had arrived.

The tourist family. Great, I thought.

A few moments later, Carlo hurried into the reception area.

"*Ciao*," Carlo said, a smile wreathing his face, his eyes lingering on me for just a second longer than the others. I searched his eyes to see if he was trying to hide something, but I couldn't tell, and besides, just looking into his eyes made my knees feel weak. He shook hands with Phil and gave Nicole, Carrie, and me kisses on the cheeks. Carrie's face turned a bright red. My heart raced a bit at the brush of his lips on my cheeks. Take it easy, I warned myself. As long as I didn't look right into his eyes, maybe I could handle this tour without losing my composure.

Almost as if he could read my thoughts, Carlo looked at me and smiled. "I'm going to speak the English today," he said. "But please do not take it as the insult. Your Italian is excellent." Now it was my turn to feel my face turn pink.

Once in the main part of his family's factory, Carlo became more outgoing and enthusiastic. His face shone with pride as he led us through the factory.

"First, the lemons," Carlo said, gesturing toward plastic bins stacked next to the wall just inside the next door. "These are the lemons we buy from the IGP lemon growers here on the Amalfi Coast," Carlo explained. "The names of the growers you see on the crates: Fonteros, Cascano, Ferrara e Figli, and so on. We must make sure the lemons are the right kind, so that our license to produce limoncello stays valid."

"What kinds of lemons do you use?" Phil asked.

"Feminello Saint Teresa and Sfusato Amalfitano, mostly," Carlo said. "They have a thick, waxy skin and have just the right flavor for the limoncello."

"What happens if you have the wrong lemons?" Nicole asked.

Carlo frowned. "The inspectors will fine us and take away our license. And, the limoncello would not taste the same and stores and the restaurants might not buy it from us anymore. So, it is very important that we use the approved lemons for limoncello production."

Carrie's eyes were glued to Carlo's face. Didn't he notice that she was totally staring at him?

"Is that what you and your professor were talking about yesterday? The best type of lemons to use?" I asked, deciding that I might as well take the plunge. I swallowed hard. But shouldn't I know the truth about this secretive meeting between Carlo and his supposed professor? I couldn't bear to have suspicions about Carlo, especially Sacra Lista-related suspicions.

Carlo looked startled; his frown appeared and was gone within a fraction of a second. "Ah, yes, of course. We were discussing a new type of lemon that he is working on, a hybrid," Carlo answered.

Why were you discussing it at the end of the tourist walkway to Il Torre Clavel and not here at the factory? I wanted to ask but bit my tongue. My heart thudded. Had I gone too far in my questioning? Or had Carlos gone too far with the Sacra Lista?

"Will he be able to get it certified?" Phil asked.

"It will be a long process, perhaps many years," Carlo smiled and shrugged.

"Is it a secret lemon?" Carrie asked.

Carlo stared at her, his face inscrutable. "Why would you ask that?"

"Well, uh," Carrie stammered, turning red, "you were meeting him out away from everyone. Is it a secret lemon?"

"Carrie!" Nicole exclaimed. "Don't bother Carlo with questions that are none of your business."

"Especially when he's kind enough to show us around," Phil added. "Sorry, Carlo."

Carrie had absolutely no clue about anything sometimes, I thought, but she did conveniently ask him exactly what it was that I most wanted to know.

Carlo's face seemed to relax and he laughed. "No," he replied. "Professor Scioscia loves the view from the *torre* and he always likes to meet there. He does not come to Positano often from the university at Napoli." Turning away, Carlo grabbed one of the lemons.

"Here," Carlo said, handing me a lemon. "Smell this." He scraped the lemon with his thumbnail, brought it to his nose, inhaled, then handed it to me. "Scratching the peel releases the oils of the lemon. Do you see?" Our conversation about his professor was apparently over.

I held the waxy, heavy fruit in my hands, scraped a bit, and smelled. The pungent scent of lemon was wonderful. "It is good," I said, smiling.

"*Buono, buono*," Carlo said, enthusiastically. I handed the lemon to Nicole who scraped and sniffed and passed it to Phil. Carrie took it next and smelled it, before handing it back to Carlo.

From the hallway, we entered a huge room with a half-dozen workers dressed in aprons with bonnets covering their hair. The walls and floors were of gleaming white tile, and rows of stainless steel tables lined one half of the room. Workers peeled the lemons in swift circular motions over stainless steel bowls.

"You do this by hand?" Nicole marveled, stopping to watch a woman peel one of the lemons.

"Most of the time," Carlo replied. "There are machines that do it also and we have some of them, but the old-fashioned way is the best. The worker can feel exactly how far to peel the lemon. We do not want to peel any of the white pith, you see, or the limoncello will be bitter."

Other stainless steel tables held dozens and dozens of glass jars. When we got closer, I could see that each jar was filled with lemon peels, suspended in liquid.

"Here is the steeping in the alcohol," Carlo said, gesturing at the jars. "After we steep them, we strain out the peels and add the syrup." He pointed to a large tank fixed with some kind of a mixer attachment. "The sugar and water together make the syrup. All of these steps make up the secret of each limoncello house recipe." Carlo smiled, and a thought flitted through my mind—what other secrets was he hiding from us?

"Then, of course, we bottle the limoncello," Carlo said. "But first, the mixture must age for forty days."

"Forty days!" Phil said.

Carlo opened double doors at one end of the room, and we found ourselves in another, smaller room. "This is where we bottle," he said, gesturing toward machines that were filled with jars, with siphons running from the machines into the bottles.

"And here are our labels," Carlo said proudly, gathering up a stack of colorful labels from a table, and spreading them out in a vivid display. Another employee, slapping labels onto bottles, smiled at us. "Only limoncello that is government approved can be sold with a license in Italy. And these recipes are closely guarded, only known to the owners and perhaps the manager of each limoncello house."

"May I take some pictures?" Nicole asked.

"Of course," Carlo said, after a momentary hesitation.

"Would any of you like to try to make the limoncello?"

"Sure!" Carrie said. We walked back into the main room and Carlo found an apron, a bonnet, and some gloves for Carrie.

"Me too," I said. "Please."

Carlo looked into my eyes and smiled. "But of course," he said, in a tone that set my pulse racing.

"We'll all join in," Phil said.

Carlo instructed us all to wash our hands at one of the sinks and then, after drying them, put on the gloves. Then we put on the bonnets and the aprons.

Carlo laughed at the sight of us. "This will be a good photo," he exclaimed. "If it pleases you, I will make a photo."

Nicole gave Carlo her camera from around her neck, and the four of us posed in a goofy row, each holding a lemon and a knife.

"No one back in the U.S. will have a photo like that," Carlo promised.

We tried to peel the lemons, but I kept cutting my peel after only a single turn around the lemon. Nicole did better, and Carrie and Phil each gave up after only a minute. We laughed and joked, and Phil told a number of lemon puns. I worried that Carlo might not understand and take offence. After translating the puns, I confirmed that Carlo understood that Phil was only joking. *"Capisci che fa dei giochi di parole?"*

We took off our bonnets and aprons and gloves, still chuckling. Carlo's eyes sparkled with fun. Watching him, my heart lifted. His meeting with the professor just couldn't be about anything sinister or criminal, I told myself. Maybe professors in Italy were much better dressed than the ones in the U.S. *La bella figura* was important to all Italians, after all. Still, there was something strange about that meeting, and the two men had definitely not been pleased at our interruption.

Carlo just couldn't be involved in the Sacra Lista. Sure, he was really intense about his business, but didn't his confrontation with Giovanni about The System prove that he didn't buy into organized crime? But, if I was wrong, and Carlo *was* into anything shady, I was in trouble—I'd already fallen for him, and fallen hard.

Chapter Ten

"Carlo!" we heard a voice call. A bald, heavyset man walked through the double doors behind us.

"My father," Carlo said, gesturing.

Signor Bertolucci offered us each a handshake as Carlo introduced us all. "Ah, the American tourists," he said, a serious expression on his face. "My daughter told me you were here. I wanted to welcome you. We hope you find our small place interesting."

"Thank you, yes," Phil said, gesturing to me. "Alessandra knows a little bit about alcohol production. Her father works for a winery in California."

Signor Bertolucci's face seemed to freeze, but then his face rearranged itself so quickly that I thought I must have imagined it. "A winery? How nice," he said, with a forced smile. "Which one?"

Embarrassed, I said, "Nightingale Vintners. It's owned by a college friend of my father's. It's just a small winery. My father does the marketing and some translating." And he's undercover trying to scope out the Camorra and the Mafia in Italy and the U.S.—which, I did not say!

"Really?" Signor Bertolucci said, his gaze intent on my face. "That is what he does? The marketing and the translation? What languages does he speak?"

"He speaks a lot of them," Carrie interrupted, "including Italian, like Alessandra."

"You speak Italian?" Signor Bertolucci asked sharply.

What was wrong with that? I wanted to ask, defensively. A sudden thought struck me. Carlo hadn't said anything at all to his father about me. But then that was pretty normal for guys, wasn't it?

"Yes," I said, hesitantly. I was starting to feel uncomfortable, as if I were being interrogated by too many pointed questions. I almost expected Carlo's father to pull out a spotlight, shine it full in my face, and ask: "And why is your father poking around in Italian wineries and asking too many questions about the Camorra and organized crime syndicates?"

Carlo came to my rescue. "Alessandra lived in *Italia* until last year. Her father was in the diplomatic service," he said, first in Italian and then, politely, in English.

"Ah," Signor Bertolucci said. "Well, welcome to you all. Please ask any questions." Then he smiled a little. "Excepting, of course, about our secret limoncello recipe."

Signor Bertolucci was serious, just as Giovanni had needled Carlo about being serious. Serious father, serious son. But Carlo could be fun, too. His dad didn't seem like the fun type at all. Plus, he acted weird about my dad's business at the winery, asking me all those probing questions. And why was he so suspicious anout our family speaking Italian? I would not translate puns about lemons for Signor Bertolucci, that was for sure.

"Permit me to leave you now. I must make the business,"

Signor Bertolucci said, inclining his head politely. "*Arrivederci,*" and he disappeared back through the double doors.

"'I must make the business'?" Carrie said to me with a snicker.

"Carrie!" I exclaimed, horrified at the thought Carlo might hear her. Luckily, Carlo had walked around one of the tables to talk with one of the workers.

"What?" Carrie demanded. "Can't I make a joke?"

I sighed. "Carrie, I'm sorry, but it is really rude to make fun of someone else when they're trying to speak your language." And when *you* can't speak anything but English, I wanted to add.

"It is time to taste a little limoncello," Carlo announced, standing next to a gleaming stainless steel refrigerator. He opened the fridge doors to reveal shelves filled with bottles of limoncello. "Would it please you to taste?"

Phil grinned. "It's early, but this is special. Of course."

"We'd be delighted," Nicole said.

"Me, too?" Carrie begged.

"Only one sip," Phil warned.

Carlo opened a bottle, removed five frosty glasses from the freezer, and poured a portion of the golden liquid into each.

"*Cin-cin!*" he said, raising his glass. We raised ours, all of us clinking our glasses together. Carlo looked into my eyes, and my breathing almost stopped. Easy, Alex—Alessandra—whoever you are, I cautioned myself.

"This is delicious," Nicole enthused.

"Indeed," Phil agreed.

"Wow! Lemonade with a punch!" Carrie exclaimed. I caught her glancing quickly at her parents, who were sipping with their eyes closed, before she downed the whole thing. "Oops!" she said.

Nicole and Phil's eyes snapped open and, at the same time, they both exclaimed, "Carrie!"

Carlo was unsuccessfully trying to hide a smile. He grinned at me, and my heart rate accelerated. I smiled back.

"Sorry," Carrie said, most unconvincingly. "The glass slipped."

"Carrie, that's just not true!" Nicole scolded.

"Oh, my gosh, Mom," Carrie said, tossing her head, "sometimes you are just clueless!"

"Young lady, you've just earned yourself an afternoon in the apartment," Phil said with a sigh.

Then, I thought, if she was going to be in the apartment all afternoon, guess who would have to be with her? I almost groaned aloud.

"You are kidding me!" Carrie protested. "I'm in Italy— and you're grounding me?"

"I have some reading to do," Phil said, "so you'll have company. Alessandra, why don't you take the afternoon off?"

"Thanks," I said. Carrie's face was a study in thunderclouds. What was I going to do all by myself in Positano? I wondered. Shop? There were some cute sandals in some of the shops, but I wasn't really that much of a shopper.

"Well, then, Alessandra," Carlo said, quickly. "Will it please you to accompany me for the lunch?"

Everyone turned to look at me, and I could feel my cheeks getting warm.

"*Sì!* Of course," I managed to say. Carlo's grin was infectious, and I smiled back. "Thank you— *grazie mille.*"

Now Carrie looked really furious, but we chatted further as Nicole, Phil, and I sipped our limoncellos. I reminded myself to try and take it easy with my sipping, especially if I was going to have lunch with Carlo. The warmth of the liqueur was already spreading through my veins, and I wanted to be able to think clearly—although, just looking at Carlo made my brain go all fuzzy. That was not the limoncello's doing either.

Carlo gave us brightly colored brochures that described the factory and its history and then, with a flourish, presented Nicole with a bottle of limoncello.

"A gift," Carlo said. "It is a pleasure." He looked right at me. I figured I was about gone.

"Thank you so much, *grazie!*" Nicole said, a smile wreathing her face.

Carlo retrieved a fancy bag printed with a lemon design and slipped the bottle inside, giving it to Nicole with a bow. "For you to enjoy. Maybe not the *ragazza,*" he joked, gesturing at Carrie and with a wink at Phil.

That must have really done it for Carrie. She rudely turned her back and began wandering around, looking at the pictures of lemons and lemon groves that decorated the walls.

"Carrie, straighten up," Phil said. "Turn around and be

polite."

Carrie spun around on her heel, her face red with anger. "Fine," she sputtered.

I resisted the impulse to roll my eyes. It was so definitely not fine with her.

Carlo escorted us out. We paused in the reception area, making conversation about the weather, while Nicole browsed over some large pictorial books of limoncello and the Amalfi Coast.

A striking woman with dark hair and high cheekbones, dressed in a red pencil skirt and an embroidered blouse, walked into the reception area from a side door marked *Ufficio*.

"Ah, I see you are still here," the woman said, with a smile. She walked over to Carlo and kissed him.

Carlo smiled. "*Ciao, Mama! Quelli sono i miei amici Americani.* These are my American friends," he said.

Carlo's mother, Adrianna—looking like she had just walked off the cover of Vogue—smiled graciously at us. Phil, I noticed, could hardly take his eyes off her during the introductions and, by Nicole's peeved expression, quickly masked, I could tell she probably wanted to snap her fingers in front of his eyes. Under Adrianna's spell, even Carrie made a reasonably polite response.

"It pleases us that you visit," Adrianna said. Then, directing her gaze to me, she said, "*Carlo m'ha detto che parli Italiano molto bene*,"—Carlo has told me you speak Italian very well. "*Benvenuta a casa.*"

139

I felt my cheeks turn warm. "Welcome home," she had said. Did she mean simply welcome to their home? Or to my Italian home in general? And she used the familiar form of *tu*—perhaps because I was younger than she, but it still had its intended effect of making me feel welcome, definitely more so than I had felt upon my first visit to Sonoma.

"*Grazie tanto,*" I said. Welcome home, I repeated silently. Like it or not, I was really beginning to feel as if I *were* home in Italy, and that I'd been away too long.

Carlo glanced at his watch, and I couldn't help noticing his strong, tan wrists below his crisply rolled-up sleeves. "It will be lunch time soon; it is now after one o'clock." He looked at me, and my mouth felt dry. "Alessandra, why don't we just go to lunch from here? I will bring her home," he promised Phil and Nicole. From the corner of my eye, I saw Carrie's face morph into sulkiness.

"You can join us here, at the house," Carlo's mother invited me. "It would be our pleasure."

"Thank you, Mama, but I would like to take Alessandra to Café Positano for the view," Carlo said quickly.

"*Grazie mille per la sua gentilezza; forse un'altra volta,*"—thank you for your graciousness, perhaps another time—I said, hoping I wasn't being too forward in suggesting that I might be invited back.

We said our goodbyes, and I waved to the Cowans as they walked out the door. Surely, I would be all right by myself, wouldn't I, with Carlo? I winced, thinking about my Sacra Lista worries. But Carlo's parents were both cordial, his mom much friendlier than his dad, but that was to be expected. His sister was nice too. Then, I thought of that so-called professor and told myself I'd find out more at lunch. I was definitely falling for Carlo, but I didn't want to get myself mixed up in any dangerous crime scheme, if that's what it was. Another reason to make sure I was on my guard, and make sure I didn't spill anything to Carlo about what Dad was really up to in the wine biz.

Carlo steered me back into the main room of the factory. He smiled and gestured at the workers, busily peeling lemons and chattering away to each other in Italian.

"Is this like your father's winery?" he asked. Now that the Cowans had left, he spoke Italian.

I grinned. "In a way, but they don't peel the grapes by hand." Carlo laughed. "And it's not my dad's winery, remember? It belongs to his friend." I wanted to distance myself, and Dad, from this winery stuff.

"How many cases of wine do they produce a year?" he asked.

"I'm not certain," I answered. "I think somewhere around 30,000." I didn't want him to think I knew all about the wine business.

"So they are not that small then," Carlo said. "We are small, but we sell everything we produce."

"Well, it's certainly delicious. I can see why," I said. I loved how Carlo's eyes lit up with pleasure when he talked about his business.

"Let's go," he said, taking my hand. We waved goodbye

to his sister, who pointedly looked at our clasped hands and tried to hide a smile. Through the side door, I saw a sleek silver scooter leaning against the side of the building.

"A Vespa!" I exclaimed.

"You did not think we were going to walk all the way into town, did you?" Carlo teased. He grabbed a helmet off the handlebars, got another from a storage cabinet, and handed it to me.

"Giulietta will not mind if you wear it," Carlo said, as I fastened the helmet strap beneath my chin.

He opened the double gates leading to the street outside. Climbing on behind him, I suddenly realized that I had to put my arms around his waist if I wanted to stay on. With a gulp, I tentatively reached my arms around his muscular torso, feeling the warmth of his body next to mine, and shut my eyes. He smelled of lemons, of course, but also of a very male Carlo scent that threatened to send me into the galaxy. Could I memorize this moment?

Carlo started the engine, and we sped off. I felt as if I were in the movies, with the wind whipping around us as the bike leaned first one way and then the next as Carlo rounded corners. It seemed that Carlo's knees might skim the very ground. Carlo laughed as we zoomed around cars stalled in traffic, past tourists lugging canvas bags, and the occasional *carabiniere*, who futilely tweeted his whistle at us.

Down the Viale Pasitea we flew, and every now and then, someone would grin and shout something at us, and Carlo would raise a hand in greeting.

"You know lots of people here," I yelled, leaning forward to make myself heard over the rushing wind. My mouth accidentally grazed his ear—which had my heart racing all over again.

"I grew up here," he shouted back. "And everyone knows Bertolucci Limoncello."

We arrived at Café Positano in a skid, Carlo shutting off the engine and coasting to a stop next to the building. I'd been here at night with the Cowans, but somehow it hadn't seemed as magical to me then as it did just now.

We took off our helmets and brought them inside with us. It was Italy, after all, and stray helmets hanging on a Vespa would be fresh meat to any unscrupulous passers-by. The receptionist greeted Carlo with two kisses, and Carlo introduced us.

"Ah, yes, the American who speaks Italian," Carmela said, nodding.

Carmela showed us to a tiny table under a vine-covered trellis. To our right, the gorge plunged down precipitously, houses and tiny gardens perched on the slopes beneath us, the turquoise sea sparkling in the distance. The view was absolutely incredible—so amazing that I actually tore my eyes away from Carlo, but just for a moment. This was a better table than the one the Cowans and I had been given the previous night. Obviously, the Bertoluccis were important guests to rate a table like this.

Carlo ordered us a bottle of wine and an appetizer, and I could tell that this was going to be a typically long Italian lunch. Settling back against the green-and-white-striped cushion of my seat, I smiled at him.

Carlo smiled back, and my heart rate responded immediately. "Alessandra, I cannot tell you how much pleasure this lunch gives me," he said softly.

I could feel the heat in my cheeks and rested my chin awkwardly in my hand, looking out at the view, hoping I could distract him from noticing my embarrassment. "Thank you," I managed to choke out.

"I feel that you are unsure?" Carlo said.

"Unsure?" I answered, startled by his comment. "Unsure about what?"

Carlo smiled a slow smile that crinkled the corners of his eyes. "Unsure if you really want to be here or not," he said.

I bit my lip and looked down at the white tablecloth.

"Not want to be here in this restaurant? Or here in Italy?" I asked, playing for time, hoping a really cool answer would spring to my lips.

He smiled gently. "I think you are liking being here with me, yes?"

My cheeks still warm, I looked down at my plate.

"No," Carlo continued, "I meant not wanting to be here in Italy." In a movement that made time stand still, he reached out and lifted my chin so I had to look him straight in the eyes. "Tell me," he said, "was it hard to leave Italy?"

Unbidden, tears filled my eyes. No one had asked me this question—no one could have come this close to understanding.

"*Cara*," he whispered, as he brushed a tear from my cheek. Embarrassed, I wondered if other diners were watching my emotional display, but then I remembered—we were in Italy, and people were encouraged to show their emotions.

"Yes," I gulped, grabbing my napkin from my lap to dab at my eyes. Carlo smiled as he reached out to take one of my hands in his. His palm felt strong and warm.

"So, how is it?" he asked, quietly, looking into my eyes. "How is it to be finally back home?"

Now, I was really going to lose it. I took a ragged breath and a gulp of wine, hoping to steady myself. "I—I'm not sure," I admitted. "I am so torn."

"Torn?" Carlo asked, squeezing my hand.

"Well, because where I live now, I just have to be careful how much I talk about living in Italy." Carlo nodded as if he understood. "The other girls…they do not understand. I want them to like me, but I also need to be myself," I finished lamely.

"So why are you torn? Are you not glad to be back where you belong?" Carlo asked, leaning closer.

Could my heart burst right out of my chest? I wondered. How could I be completely honest without offending him? "But I have to go back to America. I have to be American when I go back. I have to fit into America, do you understand?"

Carlo squeezed my hand. "Alessandra," he said earnestly, "be yourself. Always be true to yourself."

The young waiter arrived with our calamari, and I felt restored enough—now that my tears had dried—to exchange light pleasantries. The waiter looked surprised and pleased at my Italian, a reaction I was getting used to.

True to yourself, I repeated silently, as I sipped my wine. Was Carlo true to himself? Did he follow the same advice that he had so kindly given to me? He had been kind, I acknowledged, kind and patient, understanding and supportive. I smiled at him and his eyes met mine in a slow, melting look. I wondered, as I struggled for breath, whether we were very high above sea level. Perhaps the oxygen was thin here, and that was why I was feeling lightheaded.

"You are right," I said. "It's just difficult."

Carlo smiled. "It's always difficult to be true to yourself," he agreed. "I want to tell you something," he said, after glancing quickly about the restaurant as if to see who might overhear him. He leaned forward in his chair and spoke softly: "Even though we have known each other only a week, I feel I can trust you, Alessandra." He looked searchingly into my eyes. "Is that right?"

My heart thudded in my chest. "I...I hope so," I stammered. What was he going to tell me that demanded my trust? I twisted my napkin in my hands and caught my breath, hoping that it wouldn't be something that would destroy this moment—or our new relationship.

Chapter Eleven

"Alessandra," Carlo said, in a low voice. "I could tell that you were wondering about the meeting yesterday." He looked at me, searchingly. "When you saw me with my... ah...professor near the *torre*?"

I felt heat flood my face again and was sure my cheeks were bright red. Carlo noticed and grinned. "Ha! I thought so," he said. Then his face turned serious. "We are having a problem, a dangerous problem at the factory," he said quietly.

"What problem?" I asked. A dangerous problem? I gulped, immediately guessing that the Sacra Lista was involved.

"We have had some offers lately to buy our factory."

"Really?" I asked. "Couldn't that be a good thing?"

Carlo frowned. "No. First, because we do not want to sell, and second, because the offers are so low. They are disgustingly low offers. We cannot even consider them, even if we wanted to sell, which we do not. Bertolucci Limoncello has been in our family for three generations. It is our family's life."

"Why would the offers be so low?" I asked, although I thought I already knew the answer. But then, if Carlo's family was under attack from the Sacra Lista, then they were not part of it. I felt a rush of relief flood through me—Carlo was not a *banditto*, after all!

"We think it is the Sacra Lista," he whispered. "They are using other people's names to communicate with us, pretending they are not who they really are."

A chill ran down my spine, and goosebumps rose on my arms. Even though I'd already suspected the Sacra Lista was involved, actually hearing the words spoken aloud made it real. "The Sacra Lista?" I repeated slowly.

"This is what the Sacra Lista does. They offer to buy at low prices," Carlo explained, "and then, when the people do not want to sell, bad things—accidents—begin to happen to the factory or the owners." He looked at me intently. "You understand? Very bad things. It is as we discussed the other night at Café LoPresti about the distributors. It is the same strategy."

I shivered. Yes, I understood.

"So then, the owners want to sell suddenly. To stop the bad things happening to them, yes? And the owners have to sell at a very low price and lose money."

Bad things happened? I remembered with a start our discussion of the previous night, the kidnapping, the attacks, the murders! My eyes widened. "Are those things happening to you?"

"Not yet," Carlo said heavily. "But we fear it is only a matter of time. That is why I met with Signor Scioscia yesterday."

"How can a professor help?" I asked.

Carlo smiled lightly before his expression again turned grim. "He is not a professor, as you probably guessed. He is the owner of another limoncello factory near Sorrento. He managed to keep his factory away from the Sacra Lista, and I was meeting with him to get ideas and advice. We cannot talk on the phone, and to meet him in the factory—or anywhere else where there might be listening ears—would be dangerous. The limoncello business, and the wine business too, are small worlds and the Sacra Lista has many ears working for them."

"How did this owner manage to keep clear of the Sacra Lista?" I asked. I didn't like the "small world" and "many ears" part, not at all.

"He has friends he can call on," Carlo said. "Friends who are very powerful in the government. They can help us, but it is a delicate matter. It is not something I can talk about—not yet, and perhaps, not ever." He looked into my eyes and shrugged. "It is Italy. It is how things work here, you know."

In spite of the warm sun on my shoulders, I shivered a little. "No wonder you were arguing with Giovanni about the Sacra Lista," I said, realization dawning. "When you said it was not only business, he didn't like hearing that."

"Yes, the LoPrestis pretend that they work with the Sacra Lista distributor because of the convenience, and the cheap goods they can get for the restaurant," Carlo said. "But it could get worse for them too. It is dangerous to be, how you say—complacent?—with the Sacra Lista. You never know what they will do next, and they always want more."

"So the LoPrestis are working with the Sacra Lista?" I asked anxiously. "Could the Sacra Lista take over all the restaurants in Positano?" I asked. Now, it was my turn to look over my shoulder. Or wineries? I wanted to ask.

Carlo shrugged. "No, it cannot happen. The Sacra Lista does not want all the restaurants, only the profitable ones. Besides, finally the government will step in if it becomes too bad." He grinned wryly and spread his hands. "Like the trash problem in Napoli. The problem becomes important when people really think it is the best thing for them to work with the Sacra Lista, like Giovanni. There is a saying here, 'truth is considered to be only whatever gets you something.'"

With a frown, Carlo leaned back and took a deep swallow of the wine. He set the glass back on the table and looked at me. "I do not mean to worry you," he said. "I feel we are, you know, *simpàtici*, and I felt that I owed you an explanation."

I blushed and ducked my head, anything to avoid meeting those eyes. Was it possible for a human to melt? If so, I was practically a puddle on my green and white cushion. But yes, he had worried me. Now I was worried about him as well as myself. Gazing out over the terraced pastel houses, tumbling down the mountainside to the sea, I wondered wistfully how a town as beautiful as Positano—and a country as warm and welcoming as Italia—could conceal such sinister events.

Taking a deep breath, I looked back up at him. He had bared his soul to me, and I felt that I owed him something in return. "Thank you, Carlo," I whispered. My mouth felt dry, but I plunged ahead. "I, too, feel that we are *simpàtici*."

I wanted to be close to him. I wanted to share with him as he had shared with me. I wanted to tell him about my dad—about his real role in the winery—and my fears for his safety as well as my own. It was hard to be afraid and feel alone in one's fear. But something still made me hesitate.

Leaning across the table, Carlo's soft lips grazed mine, and I thought I was going to truly die. "*Carissima*," he said, smiling into my eyes. "We have so little time."

I nodded, not wanting to think about leaving in less than five weeks. I hardly remembered that I had not wanted to come to Italy at all, and now, I never wanted to leave.

We finished lunch and, as he'd promised, Carlo drove me back to the apartment on the Vespa, but not before he'd taken me in his arms in front of the entire restaurant and given me a thorough welcome to *la bella Italia*—an *abbraccio* worthy of the name. Dizzily, I held onto him as we roared through the streets of Positano, resting my head against his back, reveling in the warm strength beneath his white shirt.

At the apartment, I politely shrugged off Nicole and Phil's questions, telling them I had had a good time, but was tired and wanted to nap. Phil looked at me with one raised eyebrow—the way my dad would have looked at me if I'd resisted the post-date conversation, but let it go.

"Well?" Carrie asked, bouncing off her bed. She had her journal out, but had been obviously waiting for me.

"Well, what?" I retorted impatiently—days on end with Carrie were starting to wear on me.

"Well, how hot is he?" Carrie asked, her eyes gleaming mischievously. "Did you kiss him? More than the salutes on the cheek, I mean." Her excitement about my possible romance was sweet, but I needed a break.

"None of your business," I said. "I'm tired." I lay down on my bed and turned my face to the wall, hoping she'd leave me alone.

"You did, you totally did!" Carrie squealed with excitement. "Was it good?"

I sighed and rolled over. "Carrie, honestly, he's a very nice guy. Now, I'd like to take a nap."

Disappointment flooded Carrie's face. Of course, she had a crush on Carlo too, and no doubt thought that his attentions were wasted on me—obviously I wasn't, or so she thought—as gaga about him as she was.

"Fine!" Carrie exclaimed irritably. "Just fine." She sighed and began scribbling in her journal. I closed my eyes and hoped sleep would come soon.

Thoughts about the Sacra Lista twisted and rolled through my mind, which made it hard to fall asleep. All the intrigue that surrounded Giovanni, the horror of what might happen to Carlo and his family if they continued to resist the Sacra Lista, the fear that any innocuous looking van delivering produce to a restaurant might be full of gangsters and *banditti*—if my parents knew half of what was happening to me, they'd whisk me back across the Atlantic so fast that I wouldn't be able to see straight.

I also worried about my dad's exposure. It seemed as if everyone here in Positano knew my dad was involved in the wine business. Perhaps a member of the Sacra Lista might be sufficiently curious to check out Nightingale Vintners; if they did, they might discover that Dad had been asking a lot of questions about Italian distributors and wineries. Signor Bertolucci had looked at me strangely when he found out my dad worked for Nightingale Vintners. While Signor Bertolucci wasn't involved in the Sacra Lista, it did seem to me that he knew something about my dad and the winery that he wasn't telling anyone about.

Now that I knew the LoPresti family were cooperating with the Sacra Lista, the idea of eating at their restaurant or talking with Giovanni worried me. I could hardly insist on never eating at their restaurant again if Phil and Nicole wanted to return, but I would have to be very careful to change the subject lightning fast should Ralf's winery come up in conversation at the restaurant. And it was best to avoid any and all conversation with Giovanni.

I couldn't say anything about the Sacra Lista—or the LoPrestis' involvement with them—to Phil and Nicole. They would want me to pack up and leave, and I couldn't bear to leave Carlo, not yet. So, with this tumult of thoughts whirling around in my tired brain and the warm memories of the afternoon with Carlo—which I replayed over and over in my mind—it was no surprise that I couldn't sleep. I pretended to doze, however, so at least Carrie wouldn't bother me.

I couldn't believe it when I got up from my nap and discovered that, of all the restaurants in Positano, Phil and Nicole had again selected Café LoPresti for dinner. I suggested branching out and trying another restaurant or eating at home, but Signor LoPresti had apparently promised Phil *un piatto speciale*—a special dish—that the chef would make especially for him tonight. I was not happy about the prospect of going to a Sacra-Lista-patronized restaurant, but did my best to hide it.

After a glass of wine on the balcony, a time I tried to drag out as best I could, dreading our upcoming dinner, we walked to the LoPrestis' restaurant. My heart pounded—I was going into the wolves' den with the LoPrestis. A number of people were out enjoying the evening, doing some late shopping or going to dinner. The musical lilt of Italian hung in the air, softening the harsher German and English of the tourists—of which I, too, was one, I ruefully reminded myself. If only I really were just a tourist, I lamented, instead of knowing what I knew.

As we rounded the corner to Via Vicolo Vito Savino, I saw two boys, the *scugnizzi*, astride their *motorinos*. These boys were that same two I'd seen on our first day in Positano, the day that Giovanni had accepted the delivery from Parmalat. I took the opportunity to study them closely, now that I knew the LoPrestis' restaurant was associated with the Sacra Lista. One young man was pudgy, with a double chin, and the other resembled a wolf, lean, with a pointed nose and sharp eyes. I remembered that Giovanni had been angry that the boys had been outside the restaurant when the delivery truck arrived. This recollection confused me; maybe these boys were not Sacra Lista, after all, if Giovanni didn't want them there.

Their presence, however, made me watchful. They could be purse-snatchers waiting to prey on some poor, unsuspecting tourist. I decided that I would try to steer the Cowans to the other side of the street, acting all the while like an American tourist so as not to arouse suspicions. If these boys were up to anything criminal, I had a better chance of overhearing them if they were unaware I could speak Italian.

"What a beautiful night!" Nicole exclaimed, stopping to smell potted flowers in front of a boutique.

"Mom!" Carrie exclaimed. "I'm hungry. Hurry up!"

"Let's walk on this side," I said, quickly, glancing ahead at the two *scugnizzi* on their *motorinos*. "It's not as crowded."

Phil, noting the direction of my glance, herded Nicole and Carrie to the opposite side of the street. The two kids were talking on their cell phones—one laughing, the other intent on his own conversation.

Nicole and Carrie walked ahead while Phil walked next to me.

"You sense trouble?" he asked, jerking his head in the direction of the two boys.

"You never know in Italy," I said, with a shrug. "We call them *scugnizzi*, street thugs or pickpockets, you know."

"Well, thanks for the tip," Phil said. He straightened his shoulders and glared at the two kids as we walked past them and into the restaurant.

Signor LoPresti greeted us with enthusiasm and seated us with all the usual polite comments and exchanged kisses. Did he know those two boys outside? I wondered. And, given his Sacra Lista connections, did he suspect who my father really was?

Carrie spent the first ten minutes blatantly looking for

155

Giovanni. I, on the other hand, knew I definitely *didn't* want to see him. The waiter brought our wine together with three glasses, as per Phil's request, which sent Carrie into a state of major sulk.

"Oh, seriously!" she said, gesturing at the other tables. "Look! I am the *only* person my age who is not having a glass of wine. That is so embarrassing!"

"Not tonight, dear," Nicole said calmly, giving Phil a look. "Maybe later in the vacation. We'll see how things go."

"You have a few things to prove about responsibility, young lady," Phil said. "Let's remember the limoncello."

Carrie sighed dramatically and slumped down in her chair.

Signor LoPresti brought over the chef. "Tonight, we make for you the *spigola all'acqua pazza*—the sea bass in the crazy water," he said. "I promised you we would do something special."

I tried not to meet Signor LoPresti's eyes, worried that I would give something away by accident. Come on, Alessandra, I scolded myself. Did I actually think I could read "Sacra Lista" on his forehead? Could he read "Camorra-buster's kid" on mine?

"Thank you, *grazie*," Phil said.

"That's a whole fish, I think, with the head still on, and everything," I whispered to Nicole. "I hope that's okay with you and Phil?"

Nicole nodded. "Phil is pretty adventurous," she said with a smile. "It's not for me, though. And certainly not Carrie!" She smiled at me and I grinned back.

156

We worked our way through the bruschetta appetizers—
Phil and Nicole said 'brusketta,' now, rather than 'brushetta.'
They'd asked me to let them know if they had mispronounced
anything, so I felt obliged to explain that the *h* coming right
after the *c* in Italian makes the *c* hard like a *k*. I joked that
they wouldn't ask for a Chianti with a *ch* sound like chocolate,
would they?

After a glass of Pinot Grigio, Phil leaned back in his chair
and proceeded to tell us stories about his college's history
department, when, suddenly, I noticed Giovanni's arrival. He
strode through the front door, greeting customers by name,
stopping at each table, exchanging cheek kisses, and generally
chatting everyone up.

Carrie snapped to attention, immediately brushing her
fingers through her hair and thrusting back her shoulders,
trying, it seemed to me, to make her boobs more noticeable.
I hid a smile and kept eating my lasagna. I really didn't want
to talk to Giovanni and was happy to let Carrie do all the
chatting.

I wished Carlo were with me; I felt braver, somehow, with
him at my side. I wanted to close my eyes for a moment
and savor the warm memory of our lunch together. He had
promised me that we would spend more time together in
the weeks to come. "Mr. Serious," as Giovanni called him. It
worked for me. I felt guilty that I had not been completely
honest about my dad's work but I tried to console myself
with the fact that it was not my secret to reveal—and keeping
that secret is what kept my dad safe.

"*Buona sera*, Cowans, and Alessandra," Giovanni said, stopping at our table. Phil began to stand up, but Giovanni motioned for him to stay seated. "The lovely ladies," he said, his eyes lingering on my face. I wondered if he was trying to flirt with me, or if he was suspicious of me for some reason; I didn't want to think about what that reason might be.

"How are your meals tonight? Are they pleasing you?" Giovanni asked.

"Delicious," Phil answered. "The sea bass is wonderful."

"Ah, yes, my father tells me this morning that he will make for you *un piatto speciale*. I am glad it pleases you," Giovanni said. "Is everything else all right?"

Phil, on his third glass of Pinot Grigio, had lost his customary reticence. "Well, Giovanni," he said, "to tell you the truth, we were a little concerned about the two boys loitering outside your restaurant tonight. They looked like they might be purse snatchers or pickpockets."

Giovanni's face suddenly froze. Then, collecting himself, he forced a smile. "I will see," he said smoothly. "We do not want trouble for our clientele. Thank you for telling this to me." He inclined his head and said, "*Buona sera e buon appetito.*" Turning on his heel, he strode through the clutch of diners at their tables and disappeared outside.

Phil turned his attention back to his fish.

"What was that about, Phil?" Nicole asked, popping a bite into her mouth. "What pickpockets?"

"Well, our little Italian friend here," Phil gestured to me, "noticed two disreputable looking teenage boys hanging out across the street from the restaurant. That's why we crossed the street."

"Really, Alessandra?" Nicole asked. Carrie's face turned toward me in shock.

"Our little Italian friend"—was that what I was now? Well, after my lunch with Carlo, I had to admit that I *was* beginning to feel at home in Italy again.

Chapter Twelve

*Y*ou saw real pickpockets? Actual purse snatchers?" Carrie asked, leaning forward eagerly. "How could you tell?"

"I'm not sure they were purse snatchers," I said cautiously. "They just looked a little too shady, the way they were talking on their cell phones; those *motorinos*, too, can be good for quick getaways."

"We're certainly glad you're so observant," Nicole said.

"That comes from living here and almost being a native," Phil said.

"It was just common sense," I reassured them. "And maybe it was nothing." I started to feel uneasy about this attention and thought I'd better downplay the incident, although I did wonder at Giovanni's quick-change in attitude, as well as his hasty exit.

After a cappuccino, we rose from the table, preparing to walk home. Signor LoPresti was most solicitous, but he didn't mention anything about the supposed pickpockets or the two kids outside. There was no sign of Giovanni.

The next morning after our breakfast of eggs and fruit on the balcony, I knew it was time to write in my journal. It was becoming more of a struggle to write in English, the more Italian I felt. I was feeling like "Alex" was slipping through my fingers, and I admitted that I wasn't sure I wanted to stop

160

the slide. Carlo promised he'd email me; we had no other way of communicating. He could have called on Phil's phone, but I didn't feel right about bothering Phil. Besides, this was too new. I picked up my pen and began to write.

I had a special day yesterday with Carlo. We can talk about so many things and he really cares about what he does. He even likes his studies at the university and gets all enthusiastic about the agricultural program and about his family's business. The problem is—what will happen when I leave? But I may be way off in never-never land here. Who knows if we'll even end up together at the end of the next four weeks? I can't imagine that we won't, though. It's getting harder and harder to feel American, but, if that means I can be with Carlo, I don't think I care. Right now, fitting in back in Sonoma, which used to really matter to me, doesn't seem as important as it used to, but I do have to go back…

I slid my writing journal in my underwear drawer with a sigh. Carrie might try and find it, but so what? Did I really care what a bratty twelve-year-old thought? Before I went back to the U.S., I'd have some real work ahead of me, if I kept sliding into *Italia*. Was there an "Italians Anonymous" to help me recover?

Walking into the little living room, I saw Carrie in front of the laptop, typing away, and Phil and Nicole reading books outside on the balcony. Morning sounds of vendors, early morning traffic, and bursts of Italian conversation drifted through the open French doors from the street below.

"Can I check my email when you're done?" I asked. Carrie glanced up and sighed loudly.

"Carrie?" Nicole said in a warning tone, looking up from

her book.

"Fine!" Carrie said, shutting down her email and stomping into the kitchen. She opened up the refrigerator, complaining, "There's nothing in here to eat."

"Maybe that's why Italians aren't fat," Phil commented from his spot on the balcony. "They can't store a lot of snacks because the refrigerators are so small."

I burst out laughing. Carrie made a face at me.

"Come on, Carrie," I said, "you have to admit that was pretty funny."

I could see Phil and Nicole smiling outside.

"Yeah, yeah, yeah," Carrie grumbled. "Hurry up on your email, will you? I want to go to the beach, and my jailers won't let me go unaccompanied."

"Now, Carrie," cautioned Nicole.

"Young lady," Phil said, looking up from his book, "watch yourself."

"I know, I know," Carrie said, plopping down on the sofa and grabbing a magazine.

I opened my email and my pulse beat a little faster when I saw Carlo's email address and the subject line *"Per Alessandra."* I also saw two other emails, one from each of my parents. Nothing from Morgan or anyone else in Sonoma. They were probably all getting packed for Tahoe. With a sigh, I figured I'd better be the one to start emailing, especially since I didn't want to be tagged as "the Italian who forgot all her friends once she went back to Italy."

I read Carlo's email quickly and my heart lifted. He asked

if Carrie and I would be going to the beach today, and, although he had work to do, he wanted to meet me at La Spiaggia Grande between one and three in the afternoon. The Bertolucci Limoncello cook would prepare a picnic lunch for the three of us.

Of course! Fingers flying, I emailed him back.

I answered Mom and Dad's email. Dad didn't mention Ralf or the winery. All he wrote was, *I hope you're having a great time and remembering what we talked about.* He must have meant, *remember to say nothing about what I am doing.* A little shadow crossed over my sunny morning.

What was really bad, I thought, my spirits sinking, was that now I didn't really want to be in the U.S. anymore, even in Tahoe with Morgan and my other Sonoma friends. I wanted to be right here in Positano. When I did go back—which I would have to, eventually, of course—wouldn't everyone be talking about how I'd turned down Tahoe and messed up everyone's plans? Sure, I could play the My-parents-made-me-babysit card, but wouldn't everyone secretly wonder why I hadn't turned down the nanny job? Right now, I didn't even want to think about my life in Sonoma. I signed off my emails to Mom and Dad with *Alex*, then deleted the *x*, filling in the rest of *Alessandra*. I sighed. I'd find time to email Morgan later.

"Are you done yet?" Carrie complained, looking up from her magazine. "Oh my gosh, you are writing a book!"

"Carrie," Phil began, his voice coming through the open doorway.

"It's okay," I said, quickly. "Come on, Carrie. Get your sunscreen."

"How about letting me pack you a lunch?" Nicole offered, getting up from her chair.

My cheeks got warm. "Uh, actually, we'll be meeting Carlo at the beach at lunchtime. He's going to bring us lunch," I said.

"Oh," Nicole said, looking surprised and pleased.

"He is?" Carrie's face lit up.

"Uh-huh," I said, noncommittally, though noncommittal was the last thing I felt. Actually, I could hardly wait to see him again, to feel his lips brush my cheeks, and his warm, strong hand holding mine.

"Please thank him again for yesterday's tour," Phil called from the balcony.

"Oh, yes, please," Nicole said.

Carrie and I packed up our towels and beach gear, grabbed several bottles of water, and began walking down the hill to La Spiaggia Grande. Fortunately, Carrie didn't need a lecture today from me or Nicole on proper street attire, even though she was going to the beach. Her skirt and top passed my casual inspection, thankfully. I wondered if anything else had happened on her little adventure the other day that she wasn't telling me.

Passing Café LoPresti, I noticed the *motorino* kids weren't there, and I decided to ask Carlo and if he had ever noticed them before. Positano was not exactly a big town; maybe he even knew who they were. Carrie drifted toward the restaurant entrance on our way, and I reached out to grab her arm before she actually walked inside.

"What's wrong?" Carrie snapped. "I just want to see if Giovanni is there."

Just as I'd feared, Giovanni must have seen us from inside the restaurant, because he came out to greet us. His dark curly hair was a little unruly, and he brushed his fingers through it as he approached us. Today, he was wearing a light blue shirt and grey slacks and nice shoes, rather nice for a college kid working at a restaurant. But, then, this was Italy, the land of looking good. And he *did* look good, I had to admit, despite the Sacra Lista connection. I wasn't a fan of bad boys exactly, but he was still hot.

"*Ciao!*" Giovanni called, a smile crinkling the corners of his eyes.

"*Ciao,*" Carrie replied, as she batted her eyelashes at him. What *was* I going to do with this kid for the next four weeks?

"Where are you going?" he asked, giving us both the usual two kiss salute.

"To the beach," I answered, replying for the two of us; Carrie was momentarily stunned into silence by his kiss, her face as pink as her t-shirt.

"Ah, the beach," he said. "I wish I could join you, but I have work to do here. We have a big party of good customers here tonight and my father and the chef want the food to be perfect."

"So you will shop today?" I asked, wondering if the Sacra Lista distribution trucks would come visiting again.

"A bit," he said. "Some deliveries are coming also. The usual, you know—olive oil, pasta, Parmigiano Reggiano."

"Did you find the pickpockets last night?" Carrie asked eagerly.

Giovanni smiled, and I couldn't help but wonder how someone with such a great smile could be working with organized crime. He shrugged. "I go outside to look for these kids, but I see no one. Sometimes the kids around here, they like...*radunarsi*?" He looked at me for the English translation.

"Hang out," I said quickly.

"*Grazie.*" Giovanni turned the full force of his smile back on me. "They like to hang out, as you say, because of the girls going by. No doubt, they saw you," he added, smiling at Carrie, who rewarded him with a full-on blush.

"Sure, Giovanni," I said. "Thanks for the compliment." I smiled to take any possible sting out of my answer, aware that I sounded a little more sarcastic than I had intended. I turned to Carrie. "Let's go, before we lose a good spot on the beach."

"Maybe I'll see you later?" Giovanni asked.

"Sure!" Carrie exclaimed, before I had time to respond with a diplomatic refusal. The last thing I wanted was to hang around Giovanni, worrying about every word that came out of my mouth. For all I knew, Giovanni might be passing on to the Sacra Lista everything I told him.

"*Arrivederci,*" Giovanni said with a wave as he retreated inside the restaurant.

We continued through the narrow streets, the vines growing in the trellises above our heads, shops displaying their goods hanging outside on the walls. Tourists seemed to be everywhere, languages mingling in a swirl of sound. Everywhere, I could smell lemons and every now and then the aroma of freshly-baked bread wafting out of a small *panetteria.*

At the beach, I found a spot near a small group of American kids about Carrie's age; I thought they might take some of the entertainment pressure off me. After settling down on our towels, however, I realized that these kids were alone. I couldn't understand what responsible parent would let two girls in little bikinis, and a guy in boxers—definitely not a European!—out on a beach in Italy without any adult supervision.

Carrie, glancing over at the kids, took out her iPhone. Then she put her ear buds in, lay down, and closed her eyes. Checking my watch, I saw we had about an hour and a half before Carlo was due to arrive. I took my book out of my bag and lay down on my stomach.

"Hey!" an American voice called. Looking over the top of my book, I saw a young guy approaching Carrie. "You're American, too, right?"

Carrie must have been waiting for exactly this kind of a move, because her eyes popped right open as she quickly sat up. "Hi," she said, smiling. "Yes, yes, we are. Although, she is practically Italian." Carrie jerked a thumb at me.

The kid was nice-looking, with short, blond hair. He

167

stared at me. "You don't look Italian," he said.

I glared at Carrie. "I'm *not* Italian. I'm American too."

"She grew up here and speaks Italian really well," Carrie said proudly.

"Oh, yeah?" the kid asked, turning his attention back to Carrie, who was obviously more his age. "I'm Ben." He motioned to the two girls on the beach towels behind him who were looking our way and giggling. "And those are my cousins, Georgia and Hayley."

"I'm Carrie, and this is my—my friend, Alessandra," Carrie said. I was relieved that she didn't call me her nanny. Carrie, I knew, didn't want to have a nanny, any more than I wanted to be one.

"Hi," I said. "You can call me Alex." I turned back to my book, planning to listen in to their conversation while pretending I wasn't. The fact that these kids were running around the beach alone worried me a little, and I had enough trouble managing Carrie without any other difficult influences.

"We're here for a week with my parents," Ben said. "Then we go to Rome. We're from Indiana. Where are you from?"

"California," Carrie said. She took her earbuds out and they began talking about school, sports, and movies. Ben was starting ninth grade in the fall, and the girls were going into eighth grade.

I had to smile at the change in Carrie; she tried to act older than she was, picking her words carefully and trying to drop bits of knowledge into the conversation that I was sure she hoped would impress Ben.

"I'm in track and volleyball," Carrie said. "What sports are you in?"

"Soccer and baseball," Ben answered. My cousins are into dance and that sort of stuff."

Their conversation sounded harmless enough to me, so I tuned them out and got into my book.

"Alessandra?" Carrie interrupted my reading. I had brought the latest book in a new mystery series. Just what I needed—more mystery than I already had in real life. "I'm going to go for a swim with Ben and the girls. You can see us from here."

Looking up, I saw the girls standing next to our spot, smiling. The American kids seemed as if they would be all right, even though they were unsupervised. I could still keep an eye on them from my spot on the sand. The four of them walked toward the water, laughing and talking. I liked that it wasn't hard for Carrie to meet kids. She was tough, but she did have some positives about her.

"Alessandra," a masculine voice whispered in my ear. Startled, I looked up. Carlo was casually kneeling in the sand, his face near mine. My heart raced and I scrambled to a sitting position, suddenly aware that I was wearing a small bikini and he was fully dressed. He grinned at me. "*Cara*," he said, giving me a kiss that set my pulse right into high gear. "Where is your charge?" he asked in Italian.

I pointed to the sea. "She found some American friends," I explained, answering in Italian without even thinking twice about it.

"So we have a little time together, by ourselves," Carlo said, grinning. He sat down next to me and rummaged through the basket he had brought. "I didn't bring wine, because of Carrie," he explained.

"That was thoughtful," I said. While I would have liked to share a glass with him, I knew drinking on the job was probably not a good idea. Carlo must have been sensitive to that too.

He pulled out some packages wrapped in butcher paper. "These are some of my favorite *panini*," he said. "*Capocollo* and *mortadella* and provolone."

"Carlo, before Carrie comes back, I want to ask you something," I said.

"Anything, *cara*," Carlo answered, brushing my cheek with his fingers.

"I—I was wondering," I stammered, the touch of his fingers sending a jolt through me, "if you knew anything about the two *scugnizzi* who hang around outside Café LoPresti."

Carlo frowned. "What do you mean? When?"

"The first time I saw them was when Giovanni was getting a delivery for the restaurant, and these two kids on *motorinos* show up. One of them was talking on his cell phone. Giovanni saw them and he wasn't happy about it. Then we saw them again last night, outside the restaurant. Are they pickpockets or purse-snatchers or something? Giovanni said that they like to hang around and look at the girls."

Carlo put the *panini* down and stared out to sea. "No," he said, finally. "That is not why they are there. They are the lookouts.."

"Lookouts?" I repeated.

Carlo glanced around the beach before continuing, his voice low. "They are the business part of the Sacra Lista. If the LoPrestis have a deal with a Sacra Lista distributor, they have to know that the LoPrestis are not taking deliveries from anyone else. So, they pay the *scugnizzi* to spy."

"What?" I squeaked. "What happens if the LoPrestis accept deliveries from someone else?"

"You can guess," Carlo said. "It would not be pretty."

"But what can the LoPrestis do about it?" I asked, almost dreading the answer I knew was coming.

Carlo frowned. A dark cloud now hovered over our lunch on the beach.

Chapter Thirteen

Carlo shrugged. "I am sorry, *cara*, that is the way of it. I told you yesterday, no? This is the path the LoPrestis have chosen. Instead of trying to fight it, they give in. Believe me—and you know—to fight it can be disaster, but at least you can keep your honor."

"That's awful!" I exclaimed. "You cannot go to the police? So what about your factory?"

"The police!" Carlo shook his head. "You lived in Italy, so you must remember. Some of the police are in the pay of the Mafia and the Camorra and would inform on anyone who complained, and there is a terrible price to pay for those who complain. No, it must be solved in other ways." Carlo's mouth tightened for a moment, before he said, "As for our factory, there is no news yet. Another even lower offer came yesterday from Torino." He sighed. "I feel bad for my parents. They are so worried that the factory will be sabotaged or that our limoncello recipe will be stolen and we will be blackmailed to keep it private. They are worried that we will be forced to sell the factory at a loss, or that one of us will meet with an ugly 'accident.'"

"So what will you do?" I asked. This all sounded ominous, and it felt strange to be discussing such dark occurrences on a sunny beach.

"Right now, all we can do is wait. We have contacted the person in the government whose name Signor Scioscia gave us. We hope that he can help. As I said, it is a very delicate matter dealing with the Sacra Lista and with the government."

"What about Giovanni?" I asked. "Are the LoPrestis really in deep with the Sacra Lista?"

Carlo shrugged. "I do not know. They are successful in their business, and so far, nothing seems to go wrong for them." He looked at me. "Did you meet Valentina at the LoPrestis' restaurant?" Valentina—the girl hanging all over Giovanni at the party, and the girl who definitely had not welcomed me.

"Yes," I replied.

"She is, what you say, 'connected' to the Sacra Lista," Carlo said.

"What? She's a member?" I stared at Carlo.

Carlo grinned. "No, she is not herself a member, as you say. Her father is part of the Directory, the governing council of The System."

A shiver ran through me as I sat on the warm sand. I'd hate to get on *her* bad side, I thought. But, I realized, I was *already* on her bad side. "Does she live in Positano?" I asked. With any luck, I might not run into her again.

"No," Carlo said. "She lives in Napoli but visits her aunt here."

"She really seemed to like Giovanni," I said.

"Ha!" Carlo snorted. "She likes anyone with money, and she likes the men that can get her something. Perhaps her father made her get to know Giovanni better to solidify the Sacra Lista's hold on the LoPrestis."

"That's awful!" I said.

Carlo raised his eyebrows. "She is good at playing along," he said. "I prefer girls who are real." He looked into my eyes and I swallowed hard, thinking about my own secret—and my dad's—that I was keeping from him. Should I tell him now? This could be the perfect moment.

Just then, I heard loud chattering and laughing in English and looked up to see the four kids walking toward us, dripping wet.

"Carlo, hello!" Carrie exclaimed, grabbing her towel and rubbing it through her hair.

Hayley and Georgia, in the meantime, were staring at Carlo, open-mouthed. I quite understood their reaction—Carlo was quite the sight on the beach in his crisp white shirt and tan slacks, with his dark hair, brilliant smile, and intense eyes.

Introductions exchanged, the three kids retreated to their spot a dozen yards away. I could see Georgia and Hayley glancing over their shoulders at Carlo, and I couldn't blame them.

The *panini* were delicious. Carrie bubbled over with enthusiasm as she told Carlo all about her school and her friends. I glanced over at him during one long story, and he gave me a slow smile that made my heart stop.

Looking at his watch, Carlo finally said, "Ah, ladies, I must take my leave of you. It's been," he paused and looked into my eyes, "enchanting."

I smiled back, although what I really wanted to do was give him a long kiss and a real *abbraccio*, but I helped clean up the remains of our lunch and put it away in the basket.

"Thank you, Carlo," I said. He leaned over and kissed me gently on the lips. My breath caught in my throat, and I heard Carrie gasp.

"*Ciao*, Carrie," Carlo said, giving Carrie the usual two kisses.

"Thank you," she said, blushing, and I wasn't sure if she meant for the kisses or the lunch—probably both.

Carlo stood up. "There is much to do at the factory now, with new lemon crops coming. I am afraid I won't be able to see you for a few days," he said. My spirits sank.

"Just email me, if you can, all right?" I asked, hoping against hope. I just couldn't handle the thought of being without any communication from him, even for two or three days. The prospect of being 6,000 miles away in the U.S. was something I didn't even want to think about. We had to establish a regular email connection, and the sooner the better.

"*Cara*, of course," Carlo promised, grinning. With a wave, he took the basket and walked back up the beach.

I watched him disappear into the waterfront crowds, and I saw women—from teens to fifty-year-olds—giving him sidelong glances.

Carrie's back looked as if it were getting pink. She had moved over to join her new American friends and was talking with Ben, but I knew it was time to call it a day. "Hey, Carrie, I think we've had enough sun. Let's go."

The kids' conversation stopped, and the familiar pout took its place on Carrie's face. "But, why?"

The three kids exchanged glances. Now I was the bad guy, I could see. Well, that was what I'd signed up for.

"You can make plans to meet them another day. Give them your email," I suggested.

Soon, slips of paper and iPhone contact numbers were exchanged amid much laughter and cries of, "Okay!" and "See you!"

Carrie and I packed everything up and walked across the beach to the street. It was a beautiful afternoon. The sun shone on the golden dome of Santa Maria Assunta, and the smell of lemons and gardenias was strong on the breeze. We threaded our way through the clumps of tourists, a mass of humanity intent on their own missions.

"Hey!" Carrie exclaimed, when two middle-aged ladies in white sneakers almost ran her over. "What do these tourists think they're doing? All this pushing and shoving!"

"Remember," I said, as we turned the corner to Via Vicolo Vito Savino, "not everyone who comes to Italy feels like they have to act like a guest in someone's house." Inside, I was smiling at the fact that Carrie, having been in Italy less than two weeks, was already shedding some of her American tween characteristics and becoming more polite and considerate of others.

"Yeah," Carrie said, with a giggle. "I'd like to see how some of the snotty kids at my middle school would handle all this tourist rudeness or even this Italian culture." She smirked. "Not too well, I don't think."

I couldn't resist. "Do you mean that not everyone you go to school with is well-mannered?"

Carrie burst out laughing. "You have *got* to be kidding me! It's like mortal combat sometimes." She rolled her eyes. "Don't you know what I mean?"

Sadly, I did. "Yes," I answered. "It gets a little better in high school, but still...." I let my voice trail off. There was nothing else to add. We both got it.

"So," Carrie said, as we climbed up the cobblestone streets to our apartment, "why do you always introduce yourself as Alex?"

I sighed and tried to explain.. "Now that I've moved to the U.S., I want to fit in with everyone else. There were so many things I didn't know about what it was like to live as an American. The internet and TV aren't a substitute for really living somewhere, I found out. Sure, lots of people thought it was cool to have lived in Italy, but then, some people started making too big a deal out of it—you know how people can be—" I paused and Carrie nodded, eyes wide "—and it made me feel uncomfortable. I honestly felt like a loser sometimes, so all I want is to fit in and not be noticed."

"Oh, my God," Carrie said. And then she said something that made me forgive her for just about all the trouble she had put me through in our two weeks in Italy. "You? A loser? No way!"

I smiled at her. "Yes, me. So, I decided to just be Alex, which is the English version of my real name."

Carrie's mouth formed into an O. "So that's why? You just wanted to be an American?"

"Well, yes," I admitted. I wasn't going to go into any more detail about Morgan and my worries about the trip to Tahoe, or she might think I really was a loser, after all.

"But you're so Italian right now!" Carrie said. "You are perfect here; you speak Italian so well, and you know how to act and everything. You're pretty much Italian, I think."

I held back a sigh. Maybe I was pretty much Italian— and maybe that was who I needed to be. As we passed the LoPrestis' restaurant, I heard Giovanni's voice.

"*Ciao*, Alex! *Ciao*, Carrie!" Giovanni sat at a table, under the awning at the front of the restaurant, a drink in front of him; beside him was Valentina, with a scowl on her face. Wonderful, I thought. Let's all hang out with organized crime.

"Come and join us," Giovanni called in English.

"Just for a minute," I said. "We should be going home."

Valentina tossed her hair over her shoulder, her mouth tight. Nice welcome, I thought.

"All right," said Carrie. Then her eyes narrowed. "Who's the chick with the big boobs?" she whispered.

"Valentina," I said. "She's a friend of Giovanni's." And, I added silently, connected to organized crime, the guys who kill people very slowly and leave them to die in trash barrels in back alleys.

We sat down and Giovanni ordered us each an *aranciata*.

Carrie sipped hers, silently, a frown on her face, sneaking sideways looks at Valentina and Giovanni. I stared intently at my *aranciata*, sipping it through the straw, and wishing I could disappear into its orange depths.

"Giovanni tells me that your father owns a winery," Valentina said, her eyebrow arching. "In California. Is it a big one?" Her eyes bored into mine.

Suddenly, I felt very cold. I took my hands off the icy glass in front of me and put them in my lap. My heart pounded so hard that I was sure everyone at the table could hear it.

"N-no," I stammered. If only I could sound confident and nonchalant. "He doesn't own one. The winery he works at is very small."

"Oh," Valentina said smugly, leaning back in her chair as she draped one braceleted arm along the back of Giovanni's chair. From her expression it was obvious that she was relegating me to the "loser" side of her mental address book. At least I hoped that was what she was doing with that information. Maybe all she wanted, after all, was to humiliate me in front of Giovanni, to show me up as the daughter of an unimportant person—not to pry into Dad's business. What *I* wanted to say was, "And what does *your* father do?" That question would have earned me the *malocchio*—the evil eye—from her, for sure.

Giovanni glanced at Valentina for a moment and then said to me, "Do you make the tour of any wineries here?"

"Me? No," I answered. "I don't really have any interest." This conversation was taking a turn that was making me really uncomfortable. How could I change the subject?

"Your father, he does not want you to go and make the pictures of Italian wine-making?" Giovanni asked, leaning forward. "He is not wanting to know about the Italian wineries? Your father, he is Dave Martin, no?"

I froze. How did Giovanni know Dad's name?

"Yes, I mean, no," I said, trying to sound casual, though my heart was pounding, and my mouth was suddenly dry. "I'm sure he could get all the pictures he wanted from his friends here in Italy, if he wanted any, that is. He is in California, so that is what he thinks about—California wines, not Italian wines. He doesn't care about tours in Italy." My words tumbled out too fast. I didn't dare ask Giovanni how he knew Dad's name. I was afraid to hear the answer. This conversation was turning into my worst nightmare.

Giovanni turned to Valentina, who had pulled a lipstick brush and mirror from her expensive designer bag and was busy coating her pouty lips with a fresh coat. "Remember, Alex and her family used to live here for many years. They speak fluent Italian. They know what it is like in *Italia*. I am sure your father is still keeping current with the Italian wine industry, no?" Giovanni asked, with a half-smile turning back toward me. "He does not want you to make the tours and take the pictures?"

"No," I said quickly, hoping against hope that I would be believed. "He has no interest."

"Hmph," Valentina said, and snapped her compact mirror shut with a snap. I saw her exchange glances with Giovanni.

Now, I was terrified. They *knew*. Or had they guessed?

"But Alessandra, we did take a tour of Carlo's factory and my mom took pictures, remember?" Carrie blurted out, looking up from her drink, totally oblivious to the undercurrents of tension. She smiled proudly. Great. This kid always wanted to be included in conversations and to be thought older than she actually was. I could understand that, but her comment was exactly the wrong thing to say, at exactly the wrong time, and to exactly the wrong people.

Giovanni's eyebrows raised. "Really? I did not think the Bertoluccis make the tours."

"We wanted to see a real limoncello factory; well, Alessandra and my parents did," Carrie said.

Oh, be quiet, Carrie! My mouth felt dry, and I raised my trembling hands to the chilled *aranciata* and took a gulp.

"Carlo is making the cause of Italian-American friendship," Giovanni remarked to Valentina. "This could be interesting." She laughed unpleasantly. Typically, I would have wanted to say something that would really trash her, a witty comeback or a snarky comment, but all I wanted was to be completely invisible. We had to get out of there as quickly as we could, without arousing any further suspicion.

"Why do you call her Alessandra?" Giovanni asked Carrie. "She wants to be called Alex."

Carrie blinked. "Um…" She looked at me in a mute appeal for help.

"The Cowans are family friends," I said, into the uncomfortable silence, "and that's why they call me

181

Alessandra, which is my real name, what my family calls me. My school friends all call me Alex."

"You—or they—do not like the Italian?" Valentina asked. If words were tools, hers would have been ice picks. "Speaking Italian. Living here in Italy. Your father in the wine industry. It doesn't make the sense that you want to call yourself Alex, American-style, instead of Alessandra. Why do you do this?"

"Alex is just shorter," I replied quickly, so eager to be gone.

Giovanni shrugged and smiled. I rapidly finished my *aranciata* and reached for my wallet out of my not-designer bag.

"No, I insist," Giovanni said, making a dismissive motion with his hand. "You are my guests."

"*Grazie mille,*" I said.

Valentina replied, "*Piacere,*" but her blank stare gave the lie to her word, "pleasure." She felt no pleasure at our meeting, I could tell from her condescending manner, unless something we had said about wineries and tours had given her important information, information that she and her Sacra Lista father, or Giovanni, could use in some horrible way. I hoped not, with all my heart.

We left the restaurant, my palms sweating over what I felt had been a narrow escape. Valentina had asked why my dad wasn't interested in Italian wineries. I wracked my brain, but I couldn't remember ever telling Giovanni Dad's name. How did he come to know it? This was awful.

"Wow, she was a bitch," Carrie said, as we walked away.

I laughed, a much-needed laugh that felt good after all the tension I'd felt. We gave each other a high-five, and Carrie giggled.

"Seriously, she was so into Giovanni and was really jealous of you," Carrie said.

"Well, she doesn't need to be," I answered. If only Carrie knew!

Chapter Fourteen

The next few days passed by with a side trip to Praiano for Phil to check out the fortified guard towers, and to Amalfi—both of which necessitated trips on the fearsome Nastro Azzurro and were accompanied by plenty of shrieking from Carrie. The gorgeous scenery rolling by, however, did nothing to distract my thoughts from Valentina and Giovanni, and our conversation about Dad and the winery, and his supposed interest in Italian wines.

After our Amalfi trip, Phil drove the car back into the *parcheggio*. Carrie was sunburned, having forgotten to put on sunscreen while wearing a tank top, Phil and Nicole were tired from driving and taking notes on their research, and I couldn't wait to get in the shower and get some peace and quiet.

"*Signore, Signora, attenzione,*" the *parcheggio* guy pleaded, worry etched on his face.

"*Cosa sta succedendo?*" I asked. What's happening?

In relief, the attendant turned to me. "*I carabinieri sono qui—alla spiaggia. Per piacere, non andranno la, o vicino laggiù. Le strade sono fermate.*"

"What is he saying?" Phil broke in.

"The *carabinieri* were at the beach," I answered reluctantly. "The streets are closed"

"Why?" Nicole asked. I glanced at Carrie, a mixture of excitement and dread crossing her face.

"*Perché?*" I asked the attendant.

He shrugged. "*Probabilmente é il solito modo di fare. C'é un corpo fu spinto dale onde sulla spiaggia stamattina.*"

A dead body washed up on the beach this morning! The very beach we'd been to yesterday! "Probably business as usual," the attendant had said. It was *usual* to have a body wash up on the beach? And he used the dreaded word I'd heard too often—"business." It wasn't too hard to guess exactly whose "business as usual" this was.

I went cold. It wasn't Carlo, was it? Was this one of the "bad accidents" he had mentioned might happen? Quickly, I asked him, "*Chi é? Qualcuno di qui?*" Who is it? Someone from here?

"*No, Signorina. Nessuno di vicino.*" No one from around here. Guilty relief washed over me—it wasn't Carlo.

"*Grazie mille, signore,*" I said, and the attedant smiled in relief. He probably figured I could smooth things over with *i turisti americani* and save the local economy.

Phil, Nicole, and Carrie were staring at me during this exchange. Now that I knew what was going on, the *bee-boo-bee-boo* two-toned horns of the *carabinieri* vehicles I'd heard echoing up and down the streets made sense. One of them passed by us, its blue and white lights flashing, the two officers leaning forward, intent on their mission.

"What's going on?" Phil asked, his frown echoing his stern tone.

"Weren't those cops?" Carrie asked, eyes wide as she followed their progress down the tiny street, suddenly forgetting how crabby and tired she'd been all the way home from Amalfi.

"He said that the streets are closed going down toward the beach, so don't go that way. Luckily, we don't have to."

"Why?" Nicole asked. "Was there an accident?"

"Umm, yes," I said. They would find out, sooner or later, and it was probably best coming from me. I just didn't want to explain the entire structure of Italian organized crime or have to make mention of the dreaded Sacra Lista. I glanced at Carrie, quickly, and then at Phil and Nicole's worried faces. "A body washed up on the beach."

"My God," Phil said, who never swore.

Nicole put an arm around Carrie and squeezed her tightly.

"A murder?" Carrie asked, her face excited as she twisted away from Nicole.

"It could have been a drowning," I said, knowing that if the *parcheggio* man said "business as usual," *no one* thought it an accidental drowning.

"Can you find out more?" Nicole asked. "It's safe to be here in Positano, isn't it?"

"Of course," I said, lying through my teeth—as long as your dad wasn't investigating the Camorra, and your favorite restaurant wasn't connected with the Sacra Lista, and your boyfriend's family business wasn't being threatened by organized crime.

"What's this all about, Alessandra?" Phil demanded.

Time to tell the truth. "The attendant said it was 'business as usual.'" I shrugged. "That means it's probably some contract killing for some organized crime group."

Nicole turned white. Carrie almost jumped up and down with excitement. "Who? Who's the dead guy? Why'd they kill him?" she asked.

"We'll probably never know," I replied cautiously. "It's probably someone who was murdered in Naples." Although privately, I thought it unlikely that the tides would bring a body all the way around the Sorrentine peninsula from Naples to Positano.

"When you lived here, did this kind of thing happen often?" Phil asked, a frown creasing his forehead.

"Uh-uh," I said. "Not really. I wouldn't worry about it. They don't have anything to do with tourists," I added. "It's Mafia business." Listen to me, I thought wryly.

"You don't think we should go back to the U.S.?" Nicole asked, putting a protective arm around Carrie, who shrugged it off, frowning.

"No," I said. "Don't worry."

"Well, we'll just have to be careful," Phil said. "Thank you for translating, Alessandra."

"Sure," I replied. As if "being careful" would prevent anyone being nailed by the Sacra Lista.

We trooped back down the hill, avoiding the closed streets, and dodging passers-by who looked as if they were rushing toward the beach to watch the drama. People were the same everywhere; the lure of a train wreck was international.

Once safely back in the apartment, I showered and dressed, thankful to have some quiet time, while Phil and Nicole went out for a pizza to bring home. Carrie fastened herself to the keyboard of Phil's laptop, no doubt emailing all her friends about dead bodies in the surf and Mafia murderers. And she had thought she was in for a dull small-town vacation!

I found it hard to settle myself, though. The body on the beach made it clear how fragile everyone's existence was here—Carlo's and even mine, if the wrong people knew about Dad. And, I was afraid they already did. Dead bodies were usually a warning to someone. We were all vulnerable, and there was no way of knowing when or where the Sacra Lista would strike next. I took a few deep breaths and closed my eyes.

As much as I wanted to tell Carlo everything, I worried that my confidences would put him in jeopardy. Then *he* might end up on the beach. I swallowed hard, closing my eyes against a vision of Carlo's lifeless body in the surf, his eyes dull, his hair thick with salt, his skin gray… Stop! I shook my head to try and clear it. I wondered if, having heard about the body, Carlo would have sent me an email. He'd have to have heard about the body already; it had washed up in the morning's tide, so everyone in Positano had had all day to gossip and guess.

"Hey, Carrie," I asked, walking into the living room. She didn't look up from the screen and her fingers were racing over the keyboard. "Do you think I could email for a little bit?"

"Yeah," she replied. "So, what do you really think was happening with that dead body on the beach?"

I shrugged. "Well, it could be most anything."

Carrie's eyes gleamed with excitement. "If it was the Mafia or somebody like that, why would they kill someone? Was it for revenge or something?"

"I think you've watched too many Mafia movies," I said. "Who knows?"

"Well, if you find out anything, please tell me! My friends all want to know. They think it's so cool."

I bet they do, I thought. Thinking of all the Carrie-clones back in Sonoma *oohing* and *aahing* over a Mafia murder would have made me want to smile, if it hadn't been about such a grisly subject, or a subject that hit so close to home. Who would be the next victim? I tried to stifle a shudder.

"Sure," I said aloud. Over my dead body. Hopefully not my *real* dead body.

I logged into my email and scanned the inbox. I'd received several emails from Carlo over the last few days, always apologizing for not seeing me. He was so thoughtful, and had such integrity—in addition to his awesome good looks and his skillful kissing technique! I couldn't believe a week had gone by since he'd first kissed me; it seemed like only yesterday.

Another message had arrived from Carlo earlier that afternoon. Opening it, my face warmed at the thought of being close to him, even in cyberspace. The email contained the usual pleasantries about what he was doing at the factory

189

and what news there was for limoncello producers, but at the end, he wrote: *You know of the accident on the beach. We will speak about it later, when I will be so fortunate to see you again. It will be only a few more days and then the lemon crops will be in.*

I had so many questions, but they'd have to wait. The internet seemed like too public a place to be asking questions about organized crime, either in English or Italian. Meanwhile, I needed to email Morgan and try to fix things up, especially if I wanted to fit in when I went back. I took a deep breath and began typing.

Hey, Morgan—How is Tahoe? I'm so sorry I'm not there with you and everyone. Italy is good.

I stopped typing and looked at the last sentence. *Italy is good.* Italy—and Carlo—were awesome. That probably wouldn't go over too well in Sonoma. But, the Sacra Lista was definitely *not* awesome. And the fact that Giovanni knew my dad's name was also *not* awesome. Dead bodies were *not* awesome. What in the heck would Morgan and everyone think about that? It was like a movie—a bad, scary movie—and I was stuck in the middle of it.

But, I miss everyone. I wish I were there with all of you. Let me know what's going on.

Then, I carefully typed my name. *Alex.* Pushing send, I logged off. With any luck, I would get an answer in the next few days. Or not.

Naturally, that night, I dreamed in Italian, just as I did every night now. Restlessly, I turned in my bed, trying to push the scrawny little pillow into a comfortable position, but thoughts of the Sacra Lista and bodies washing up on the beach made me throw the covers off and on all night long.

Writing in my journal was usually a great way to work things out, but my journal pages had been blank for the last few days, and I couldn't bring myself to write in English. Guiltily, I knew I didn't want to, because, in some goofy way, I was afraid that writing in English would mean I'd be separating myself from Carlo. Besides, I most definitely could not write anything about the Sacra Lista or The System or anything remotely resembling what was actually happening to me, or the things that I was most worried about. Writing in Italian was out of the question. I knew my Italian self was already taking over, and it was increasingly a struggle to stay American.

"Well," Phil announced during our balcony breakfast, "we've been here almost three weeks. What do you say we take a day trip to Paestum, get out of the Positano drama, and stay in Salerno on the way back? Then we can take our time in Paestum."

"That sounds nice, Phil," Nicole said. "You know I'm really anxious to see those Greek ruins. They might be good inspiration for some weaving that I'm thinking about."

"What's Paestum?" Carrie asked.

I hated to miss seeing Carlo those two days, but I knew Phil and Nicole would never let me stay alone in Positano. And I did have a twinge of fear that some Sacra Lista thug might snatch me right off the street, or break into the apartment at night, press chloroform over my nose and throw me in the trunk of his car. Then, he would threaten my dad.

I felt everyone's faces turn toward me, and I looked up from my yogurt. "Um, sure," I said.

"You've probably been there plenty of times, Alessandra," Phil said, "but we'd sure appreciate your help translating."

"Of course. No problem," I said. I appreciated the fact that while I was working for them, Phil and Nicole always made me feel as if I was part of the family.

"But Alessandra's going to miss seeing Carlo!" Carrie teased me, which, unfortunately, made my cheeks turn warm.

"Now, Carrie, that's none of your business," Nicole said, with a smile at my hot cheeks.

Carrie slumped down a little in her chair. "Fine," she mumbled. "It was just a joke."

I gave Carrie a reassuring smile. She didn't mean any harm.

"I'll make a reservation online. Maybe Carlo can suggest a good hotel, Alessandra?" Phil asked. "We could probably make it there and back in one day, but I don't like the thought of driving the coast road late at night."

"Good call, Dad," Carrie said.

After breakfast, I checked my email and was delighted to find one from Carlo in my inbox.

Cara, I read in Italian, *please be my guest tonight at dinner at our favorite Café Positano. I will call for you in my Vespa at eight o'clock. Affezionatissimo, Carlo*. Most affectionately! My heart lifted.

Fingers tapping over the keyboard, I answered him in Italian. *Of course, and thank you! We are going to go to Paestum for a day and stay overnight in Salerno. Can you recommend a place to stay?* My fingers hesitated for an instant. Would I sign off *con mille abbracci e baci*—a thousand embraces and kisses? I blushed. Instead, I wrote: *Affezionatissima, Alessandra.*

Within a few minutes, an answer popped up in my inbox from Carlo. *Hotel Corona, should be perfect. Aff. mo Carlo*

I gave Phil the information and my seat in front of the computer, so he could make the hotel reservation.

"What's on for today?" Carrie asked Nicole, who was washing the last of the breakfast dishes.

"I need to get some work done," Nicole said. "Your dad is in the middle of some preliminary research on the internet. He may want to visit a few sites he finds." She smiled at Carrie. "You and Alessandra are on your own. You've been good sports the last few days while we've dragged you around."

Carrie looked at me. "I'll email Hayley, Georgia, and Ben and see if they want to meet us at the beach. They had a paddle ball game organized…that would be fun, wouldn't it?" she asked.

"Are those the kids from Indiana that you met on the beach?" Phil asked, looking up from the computer. "It'll be safe on the beach, won't it?" he asked me.

I nodded. The beach wasn't where murders happened, it was just the place where the murder victims ended up.

"Yep, they're the Indiana kids. Can I use the computer?" Carrie asked, nuzzling her dad. "Please, oh please, before they make plans already?"

Phil grinned. "Here you are," he said, getting up from the chair.

Arrangements were made to meet an hour and a half later at La Spiaggia Grande. Carrie and I went through our usual routine of packing towels and sunscreen and water, as well as some *panini* for lunch.

"No catered lunch today?" Phil asked, his eyes twinkling.

I reddened a little. "Um, no. Carlo is busy with lemon producers right now, but he wanted to take me to dinner tonight, if that's all right?" I asked.

"No problem," Phil said. "Please just let us know where you're going."

The American kids were already at the beach, their towels spread in a circle, and they'd brought lunch too. I quickly realized that I was essentially babysitting them all, and again wondered what their parents could possibly be doing—hadn't they heard about the body that had washed up on the beach? Carrie and I spread our towels to join the circle.

The kids grabbed the paddles and rubber ball and jogged down to the hard-packed sand near the water. Soon they were shrieking and laughing as they walloped the ball back and forth.

I lay on my stomach, reading, with my head facing the water so I could keep an eye on the kids. They seemed nice enough, but you never knew.

From behind me, I heard two men speaking in Italian.

"You are late," one muttered.

"Business," said the other.

"It's always *business*. But they will be sorry."

"Yes," the first said. "They will be as sorry as that poor fool found yesterday."

I stopped in the middle of turning a page, breath caught in my throat, immobilized by fear.

"I heard about the plan," the second man replied. I could hardly stop myself from turning around to see who it was..

"It is the winery idea," the first said. "That is the one. That will work."

I froze. Then I realized that they didn't know who I was. I looked just like any other young American tourist. In a million years, they would never think I could understand every word they said, much less understand what they were referring to. The winery idea? I felt as if ice water was running through my veins.

"We cannot talk here," the first man muttered. "Too many ears."

"Tourists, only tourists," the other answered. But then they both shut up and continued their walk, not five feet in front of me, across the sand toward the walkway to La Spiaggia Fornillo. Heart racing, I stared out at the ocean. Tranquil waves lapped the shore, as they had done before the Normans and before the Moors. What I had just heard was so at odds with the sunlight dancing on the waves and the cheerful calls of the beachgoers that I felt as if I were in a major disconnect.

I sat up, pretending to look for Carrie, as I shaded my eyes with one shaky hand and glanced at the retreating men, now thirty metres away. One of them was talking on a cell phone.

The not-so-veiled threats I had just heard chilled my blood despite the hot Italian sun that beat down upon my back. I wondered fearfully whether the men meant to harm Carlo, the Bertoluccis, or even my dad. Was their plan to further entangle the LoPrestis in the Sacra Lista agenda? Or, did it have something to do with Carlo and his family's limoncello factory? They had had little success in purchasing the Bertolucci factory at rock-bottom prices; did they now intend to harm one of the family?

But what really chilled me to the bone was the reference to a winery. Valentina and Giovanni knew my dad's name. They knew he worked for a winery and had wondered about his interest in Italian wineries. My mouth felt dry.

While I was the only person that *I* knew of around here who had a winery connection, wineries in Italy were a dime a dozen. It was likely that the winery they were talking about wasn't Ralf's at all, but some other Italian winery. Even the mention of the word *winery*, however, scared me to death given the secrecy that surrounded my dad's covert operations.

Taking a long swallow from the water bottle, I tried to clear my head. Then I shut my eyes, laid my head on the hot towel, and hoped that a nap would help bring some clarity to my situation.

The rest of the afternoon passed in a haze of sunshine, salt spray, and laughter. Ben, Georgia, and Hayley were good kids, so perhaps it wasn't all that surprising that their American relatives let them go to the beach alone. We talked about the differences between Indiana and California, and those between America and Italy. They deferred to me as the expert on all things Italian, even though I tried to tell them I was just as American as they. With a sigh, I realized that I sounded less and less convincing, even to my own ears.

Before we knew it, the sun was low on the horizon, and plenty of tourists had already packed up and left. It was time to go. I couldn't wait for eight o'clock and Carlo. Even though Carrie kept trying to delay our departure, thinking of questions to ask her new friends, I managed to hurry her up and we said our goodbyes to our companions and walked back up to the apartment.

"Please thank Carlo for his hotel recommendation. I got us reservations at the Hotel Corona. It looks very nice," Phil said.

"Sure," I answered, thinking I'd like to give Carlo a nice, lingering kiss to thank him, but wasn't going to share *that* with anyone.

Carlo knocked on the door exactly at eight, and Phil let him in. I felt a little funny hearing their "hellos" from my bedroom; my heart was a-flutter with the idea that this was just like a real date, after all. When I came into the room, Carlo and Phil were laughing together.

"*Che bella!*" Carlo said, his eyes twinkling. How could I keep breathing on my own? Did I have to focus and concentrate so I wouldn't forget to take a breath during dinner? Carlo was wearing a pale pink dress shirt, black slacks, and sleekly styled black leather shoes. His hair, mussed from his helmet, was a little unruly, and a smile lit up his face. I couldn't believe that I had him all to myself tonight.

We sat at the same table at Café Positano that we had had a few days before, the one with the spectacular view of the harbor. Looking over the terrace from our table, I could see the lights winking on the mountainside, and the moon cast a silver sheen across the bay. The view would have taken my breath away—except for the fact that I was already breathless, thanks to the young man who sat across the table from me.

Taking my hand, Carlo gazed into my eyes. "*Cara*, you look so beautiful tonight. But, of course, you look beautiful always."

The warm strength of his hand sent waves of heat racing through me. "Thank you, Carlo," I managed to answer. "You look nice, too." That was an understatement.

The waiter brought us wine and water, and we talked about my days on the beach with Carrie, and Carlo's responsibilities at the factory. I wanted to ask him about the conversation I'd overheard on the beach, but knew that I could not. I could not reveal the reason for my fear, nor could I tell him about my dad and his investigation of the Camorra. And, I thought, melting under his gaze, I did not want to place Carlo in further danger. But, at least I could ask him about the body.

"Carlo, do you know anything about the body that washed up on the beach?"

He frowned, glanced around the crowded restaurant, and

leaned closer to me. "It is, as we say, a warning," he answered.

"To whom?" I asked, a shiver running down my spine.

Carlo sighed. "My father and I do not know. It might be a warning to us."

I grabbed his hand and he squeezed it, his strength sending warm pulses through my body. "Carlo!" I exclaimed. "Are you in danger?" Was I?

He shrugged. "Perhaps," he said. "But we have to accept it. It is just a fact of life. Besides, we do not know yet to whom it was a warning. There could be many people who were targeted—even Giovanni—if he is thinking about not cooperating with the Sacra Lista anymore. Or to someone we do not know. The body could even have washed up on the wrong beach and was supposed to be in Praiano, or somewhere else. You know they take the body out to sea and let the tides take it to where they want the warning to be found. It could be a mistake that it washed up in Positano."

Looking into his warm eyes, filled with concern, I decided I didn't want to darken this special evening anymore. So I changed the subject and began asking him lots of questions, not just because you were supposed to do that with guys, but because I was really interested in everything about him. He loved talking about the limoncello factory and I loved to listen to him talk about it. Carlo told me that the Bertolucci family had worked at the factory for two generations; he described the different techniques they were using to improve limoncello production. Carlo had given a lengthy explanation about the pros and cons of different varieties of lemons, when he stopped and looked at me. "You know, *Cara*, I love talking with you. No one else is so interested in what I do. You are amazing." He smiled a long, slow smile. My mouth felt dry.

"I think it is so interesting," I said. "Most of the guys in the U.S. don't have much to say." And besides, I wanted to add, I just want to know everything there is to know about you.

"I cannot believe how we have become so close, so soon," Carlo said. "It makes me so happy. I think we are, how do you say in English, the soul-mates?"

"Yes," was all I could manage to choke out. "It makes me happy too," I added, my heart pounding so loudly that I thought he must be able to hear it across the table, in spite of the noise in the restaurant and the loud laughter of the other diners.

Now, keeping the truth from him was making me really uncomfortable, and suddenly I knew that if I was going to have an honest relationship with him, I had to say something to him soon about my dad, what he was really doing at the winery, and the veiled threats I'd heard on the beach that morning. I felt so torn; Carlo had been so honest with me and I had hidden so much from him. Lifting my glass of wine, I took a sip. Right now, I just wanted to live in the moment, as I'd heard Mom say.

Tomorrow, I'd figure out how to tell Carlo the truth about what Dad was doing. I had to say it just right, so he'd understand why I'd not said anything before. Surely,

I could trust him. After all, he had trusted me with his family's secret about their factory. Besides, if he knew about Dad's investigations maybe he could help Dad in some way. After overhearing that conversation on the beach, and after Valentina's and Giovanni's cryptic comments, I knew I needed to talk to Carlo. The more information Carlo had about the Sacra Lista, the better he would be able to take care of the Bertolucci Limoncello problem. I didn't want Carlo hurt, or dead.

"My father and I have to go to the university in Napoli in two days," Carlo said. "We have a lemon growers' seminar to attend. Many important people will be there."

"Three days?" I squeaked. "But…"

As always, Carlo seemed able to read my mind. "Yes, Alessandra," he said, shaking his head. "When you get back from Paestum, I will be gone. But," his awesome smile crinkled the corners of his eyes, "as soon as I come back, we will be together." He reached out a hand and took one of mine in his. "I promise you this. We will be together, in a very special way."

This time, there was no stopping the red that colored my face. "Thank you, Carlo," I whispered.

"We have not much time left together," he said, his voice deepening. "But I am thinking that our future is ahead." He looked at me earnestly. "Fate cannot keep us apart. This, I know in my heart. Perhaps you can study in Italy? Perhaps I can go to California and study the wines?" He smiled.

I felt dizzy, and it wasn't from the glass of wine. Carlo

thought we had a future! Reality check, Alessandra-Alex, I cautioned myself. We lived thousands of miles away; we couldn't have a future together, could we? No, I didn't want a reality check. I wanted Carlo.

We enjoyed our dinner and shared a glass of Bertolucci Limoncello afterwards.

"Compliments of the house," our waiter said with a smile, as he set the frozen glass of liqueur on the table in front of Carlo.

We sipped our limoncello, and I savored the fact that my lips were touching the glass where his had touched. I never wanted this night—or my time in Italy—to end.

We drove slowly through the cobbled streets, the warm Italian air caressing my face. I snuggled next to him on the back of the Vespa and fantasized I could feel his heart beating. He smelled like lemons, fresh and clean. When we got to the apartment, he turned the Vespa off and helped me off the back. Then, without a word, he took me in his arms. If people could melt, I thought, sinking slowly into his strong embrace, I would be a little pool of Alessandra on the cobblestones.

After a long, slow kiss, he tipped my face up with his hand under my chin. "You are so beautiful, inside and out, Alessandra," he said. "I want you to know that I do want to be with you." My heart pounded in earnest now. "But," he continued, "I care for you too much to disrespect you. Only when it is right," he said, looking into my eyes. "I promise you. And someday, it will be right."

My mind blurry from all of the emotions that had swirled around me and swept me up this evening, I couldn't phrase a question, as in, "When? Before I leave?" But "someday" sounded even further off than that. Which was fine—I wasn't ready yet for anything like that, even with Carlo. But, the thought of being with Carlo, his arms around me, gazing into his dark brown eyes, feeling his warmth, his strength...

"As soon as I come back from Napoli, I will see you," Carlo promised, when we stood in front of the door to the apartment. I handed him my key. He turned it in the lock, brushed his lips against mine one last time, and said, *"Buona notte, Carissima."*

The lights were out in the apartment, except for one small light in the kitchen. I turned it off, amazed that I could perform such a simple task when I felt as if I'd been in a dream all evening long.

I got ready for bed and slipped under the covers. How could I sleep with my heart racing? Alex, Alessandra— whoever I was...what had I gotten myself into? *Il cuore é Italiano*, my heart was Italian, I finally admitted to myself.

I couldn't find any other answer. And I didn't want to.

Chapter Fifteen

The next morning, we lugged our overnight bags past Café LoPresti to the *parcheggio* to pick up our car for our trip to Paestum. Remembering Valentina and Giovanni's chilling insinuations, I walked as quickly as I could, turning my face the other way, hoping we could avoid seeing Giovanni or his father.

Carrie, of course, slowed way down, poking along. When I glanced back at her, she was gazing longingly through the plate glass windows of the restaurant.

"Carrie!" Phil called.

"Hurry up," Nicole urged her.

"*Ciao*, Alessandra. *Un momento!*" A familiar female voice stopped me in my path. In dread, I turned around. "*Cioé*, Alessandra!" Valentina said from a table outside Café LoPresti, her head tilted to one side. "*Dové vai?*" she asked. Where are you going?

What do you care? I wanted to retort, but knowing what her father did, I chose the quieter road. "Paestum," I answered.

"*Andrái vedere le aziende vinicole?*" —Was I going to see wineries? Her question stopped me cold. She'd know even better than I that the area around Paestum was mozzarella country, not winery country.

Stunned, I tried to sound casual. *"Aziende vinicole?No, andremmo per studiare le rovine. Signor Cowan é professore."*— Wineries? No, we are going to study the ruins. Mr. Cowan is a professor.

I could not believe what she'd just asked me. Could it be that the U.S. government had shared news of my dad's undercover work with Italian Interpol, which then was leaked to the Camorra? How many weeks did I have left in Italy—alive?

Valentina raised her eyebrows. *"Non studia i vini? Spero che sia proprio giusto,"* she said, a little smile on her pouty lips— You're not studying the wines? I hope you're right.

If I hadn't been frozen with fear at her implied threat, and if I'd had my tennis racket with me, I could have just popped her one for attitude.

Valentina took out her compact mirror, crossed her legs in her red leather miniskirt, and ignored me as she studied her reflection. Shakily, I took a deep breath. If only I could call Dad and Mom and talk to them, but if I did, I knew they'd have me on the very next plane from Fiumicino to San Francisco.

"Ciao," Valentina said with a sneer.

I couldn't even muster enough breath to say *"ciao"* back in a normal voice, so I just nodded and caught up with Carrie.

"What was she saying?" Carrie asked, who'd hovered on the fringes of the conversation a few metres away.

"She wanted to know where we were going," I said, trying to make my voice sound casual.

"Yeah, probably so she'd know how many days she had Giovanni all to herself," Carrie said with a snort. "What was up with the red leather skirt?" she added with a smirk. "Bet she wasn't wearing underwear—not even a thong!"

I grinned and motioned for her to follow me as we hurried to catch up with her parents.

The drive to Paestum took three hours. Valentina's conversation kept running through my mind. *Why aren't you studying the wineries?* Her words echoed back and forth in my brain, unanswered questions piling on top of each other like haphazard building blocks, threatening to topple over and crash.

We made it safely all the way on the Amalfi Coast road, and then past Salerno. Leaving the low mountains behind us, we drove through flat countryside and past dozens of mozzarella factories. Scruffy-looking buffalo—who would guess they were responsible for the creamy, delicious mozzarella?—grazed on yellow, patchy grass. I was really, really glad that we weren't going to try and make it to Paestum and back in one day. It would have been way too much.

"Oh, my God!" Carrie exclaimed, looking out the window at the ruins of Paestum as we pulled into a parking space. "It looks like Greece!"

"That's why we're here," Phil said, grinning. "This part of Italy was part of Greece in the ancient days," he said in his professorial voice. "Then, after the fall of Rome, the Saracens invaded, and the Normans conquered it in the ninth century."

"I wanted to see some of the temple friezes for my work on Greek patterns. They were used as the basis for Italian regional weaving," Nicole contributed. "They are supposed to be some of the best examples of Greek art that we can see."

Carrie sighed and rolled her eyes. "Well," she said, "maybe there'll be some cute guys, right, Alessandra?" Then she looked at me mischievously. "Or is your heart taken by the limoncello guy?"

Phil cleared his throat and looked at me and Carrie. I stepped into the brief silence. "Oh, sure, Carrie. My heart belongs to Carlo." Then I giggled a little, too. I could just imagine what Phil and Nicole must be thinking: "Imagine! Alessandra and a young Italian man—just three weeks and she's a goner," and "What will we tell her parents?"

Paestum was gorgeous. I appreciated it even more than when I was younger, when Mom used to drag me along with crowds of American tourists when she was acting as a volunteer guide for the embassy's visitors. Acres and acres of austere, beautiful Greek ruins encircled us—temples, amphitheatres, apartments, and baths. Everywhere we looked was another temple, its columns perfectly symmetrical, and the friezes above, intricate and detailed.

The ruins were nearly deserted. Few visitors ventured this far into southern Italy—it was a poorer region of the country and, I reminded myself with a gulp, the Camorra was very influential here. Involuntarily, I looked around. No one was following me, were they? Come on, Alessandra, I scolded myself, cut the overactive imagination. Surely, all these people were just innocent tourists like us. I needed to enjoy the visit and forget all my worries and conspiracy theories, even though they hovered constantly on the fringes of my mind.

A few other small groups of tourists picked their way across the ancient cobbled streets, some guided by translators, others using audio-tour guides that they wore around their necks. We paid for our audio-tour guides at a window and, using our maps, turned on our guides. I turned mine to Italian, just to see if my soundtrack would be different from what the Cowans would describe. Besides, it made me feel closer to Carlo.

I sighed. One way to get closer to Carlo was to be honest with him about Dad's work. I had already decided that when he got back form Napoli, I would tell him everything, including my exchange with Valentina and Giovanni and their unusual interest in the winery where my dad worked.

We took a break for lunch at one of the little sidewalk cafes just outside the grounds. We ordered fresh *buffala* mozzarella, basil, and tomato *panini*. Phil had taken notes and Nicole had sketched during our tour, and they compared their findings as we ate lunch. Carrie had had her audio tour guide earbud in one ear and one iPhone bud in the other during the tour, so she didn't have much to contribute. It seemed that the Italian audio guide was pretty much the same as the English one, but, of course, the Italian version was more enthusiastic and complimentary about the ruins. The

Italians thought with their hearts. I winced a little, realizing that I was thinking with mine too. It felt so normal and so right to act that way, instead of always watching everything I said and did so carefully as had become normal in the U.S.

We spent the rest of the day touring imposing temples and houses reconstructed by the archaeologists. At one point, we sat on a bench and just admired the view. It was so quiet and, closing my eyes, I could imagine the hustle and bustle of ancient life, of wooden-wheeled carts rolling over the cobbled streets, vendors hawking their wares, and people in togas walking up the temple steps.

"Think about this," Phil said. "If it weren't for the mosquito, we probably wouldn't be looking at these ruins today." He made a high, buzzing sound and reached over and pinched Carrie's arm.

"Ouch! Huh?" Carrie asked. She took her earbud out of her ear. "What are you doing, Dad?"

"Got your attention, finally, did I?" Phil joked. "I just wanted you to fully enjoy the cultural experience."

"What do mosquitoes have to do with anything?" Carrie asked, pouting and rubbing her arm.

Phil cleared his throat. "Well, the eruption of Vesuvius damaged the infrastructure and drainage system of Paestum. It was already a swampy area, and the mosquito thrived and drove all the inhabitants out. So, these beautiful temples survived. Otherwise, if people had stayed in Paestum, these buildings would have been torn down and used for new construction, as everyone did in Rome and in other historic cities."

"No kidding," Carrie said. "So, good for the mosquito." She grinned.

Phil was right: Italians were good at making use of what was around them. Unfortunately, organized crime had done the same thing by taking advantage of the way things worked in Italy for their own financial gain. But why did the Sacra Lista have to pull Carlo and me into its vortex?

As the late afternoon sun began sinking, we turned in our audio guides and drove the hour to our hotel in Salerno. We found the hotel, thanks to a *carabiniere* directing traffic at an intersection, who was surprised and pleased to answer my questions in Italian.

The hotel valet took our car and we carried our overnight bags to the front desk.

"Ah, Signorina Alessandra Martin is with your party?" the man behind the marble counter asked, when Phil gave him his name.

"Yes," Phil said, surprised. He gestured to me. "This is she."

"*Scusi*," the man said. He bent down behind his counter, and brought up a vase of beautiful yellow roses. "For the young lady," he said with a smile. "She has made a friend, it seems."

Stunned, I set my bag on the floor and took the vase in both hands. I buried my nose in the fragrant roses and breathed deeply. They were yellow, like lemons, I thought. They had to be from Carlo. I opened the tiny envelope attached to one of the roses.

Manchi moltissimo al cuore. Carlo, I read. My heart misses you terribly; but the Italian didn't translate exactly that way into English. Instead it was more literally: *you are missing to my heart.* Italian was so much more a language of the heart and emotions than plain old practical English.

"Let me guess," Nicole said, smiling. "From the butcher?"

I giggled. Carrie leaned over to smell the roses. "Holy cow!" she exclaimed. "Carlo is really hot for you."

"Carrie!" Phil said, trying to sound stern, but not quite managing it.

The rest of the evening passed in a haze. I couldn't wait to see Carlo again, and already felt that I missed him dreadfully. And now I had to wait three more days until his return from Napoli. At least I could use the time to plan how I was going to tell him about Dad's undercover work for Ralf. While I longed to be with Carlo again, and wanted the hours to rush by, at the same time, I wanted the minutes to drag; after all, the date for my departure from Italy loomed over my horizon like a black cloud.

During the drive back, I kept the roses wedged carefully next to my bag, giving them a little sniff every now and then. We arrived in Positano in the early afternoon. As soon as we got into the apartment and Phil booted up the computer, I quickly emailed Carlo my thanks, hoping he would have time to read email during his seminar.

Somehow, I knew, though, that he would already know exactly how thoughtful and loving I thought his gesture. We didn't really have to explain a lot to each other in Italian or in English; we spoke the same language, the language of the heart. I had gotten emails from my old friends Caterina and Giuseppa and Maria, but I couldn't tell them about the depth of my feelings for Carlo. I wanted to keep him all to myself. How could anyone else even begin to understand what he was like, and what our relationship was quickly becoming?

That night, I dreamed that Carlo and I were embracing together in Paestum, surrounded by a carpet of yellow roses. His mouth was soft and warm, and his arms encircled me tightly. Then he gently stroked my back and feathered my neck with light kisses, sending chills through me. When I woke up, the sunlight streaming through the blinds, the roses were the first things I saw, their fragrance heavy and sweet. Somehow, I had to get a grip on myself, I thought, rolling over and burying my face in my pillow. Sighing, I got up to face another day without Carlo.

"I've missed two days at the beach and I'm losing my tan," Carrie complained over breakfast.

Phil salted his hard-boiled egg and looked across the table at his daughter. "Fine, Carrie," he said. "Alessandra? Would you mind going with Carrie to the beach? Nicole and I want to consolidate our notes and do some research today."

I nodded. "Sure," I said. There was nothing else I wanted to do—since Carlo was in Napoli.

"Thanks, Alessandra," Nicole said, reaching over and patting my hand.

Our pre-beach drill completed, Carrie and I took off

down the streets toward La Spiaggia Grande. Of course, we had to pass the LoPrestis' restaurant. My stomach tightened when I saw the two *scugnizzi* on their *motorinos* on the sidewalk outside the restaurant. They were leaning back on their cycles, laughing and talking together, oblivious to the passers-by who had to walk around them. They didn't look at all like the two guys I'd overheard on the beach; these *scugnizzi* were much younger and skinnier.

As we approached the *scugnizzi* from behind, and just as I was trying to rush Carrie past them as quickly as I could, Carrie dropped her bag and spilled everything on to the ground: lipstick, comb, magazines, water bottle and who knew what else. I groaned, wondering if she'd done it on purpose, across from Café LoPresti.

We bent down and began picking up her junk, trying to stay out of the way of the tourists and pedestrians. I could hear the two kids' conversation. Lounging on their *motorinos*, watching the traffic pass by, they hadn't noticed us. They were commenting on the girls passing by, so I did not pay much attention, until—

"*É vero!*" one exclaimed.

"*Si! É vero! Ho sentito che é ora – ora d'andare al' prossimo livello.*"

"*Non credevelo possibile. Credevo che non fosse non cóme gli altri.*"

"*Non possiamo mai sapere. Giovanni, piace essere un'uomo importante.*"

"*Si. Adesso, é lui che ci dira cosa fare.*"

Stunned, I froze in terror, the conversation playing over

213

and over in my head like a bad horror movie one was forced to watch through to the end. They spoke about someone who surprised them, someone who wasn't like the others. They said this man was going to go to the next level, that he was going to be a boss, and that he wanted to be an important man and give orders, after all. Then the part that chilled me, despite the warm sun on my shoulders, was the name they used for this "someone"—Giovanni.

I scrambled to pick up the rest of Carrie's things, shoved them into her bag, and took her arm. "Let's go," I said, trying to keep my voice level. I glanced over at Café LoPresti. I thought I saw a glimpse of Giovanni staring at me through the window. I felt sick.

We walked quickly past the two kids, who whistled when they saw us.

My heart was beating so hard that I thought it would burst out of my chest. It seemed that Giovanni was more heavily involved in the Sacra Lista than I had thought. He had become one of its very leaders! Perhaps he would now be giving orders to the *scugnizzi*—orders to harass Positano businesses? To steal, to kill? I felt as if I were walking underwater with everything around me muffled and distorted.

"Your face looks funny," Carrie said, as we turned a corner into Via dei Mulini, shaded by the overhanging bougainvillea. "Do you feel okay?"

"I guess I just stood up too fast back there," I muttered. There was no way I was going to tell Carrie what I'd heard before I told Phil and Nicole. And there was no way I was going to tell Phil and Nicole before I talked to Carlo. For sure, he could give me a sense of what was really going on. I would finally tell him everything—and what a relief that would be!—about Dad and the undercover investigations, the guys on the beach, the *scugnizzi*, and the recent exchange with Giovanni and Valentina. I shut my eyes in anguish. How I wished I'd already told him.

The next two days dragged by slowly and painfully, my sleep filled with nightmares of Sacra Lista assassins and other menacing hooded figures. Some nights, Carlo came to rescue me, and my heart lifted; in others, the Sacra Lista kidnapped me, and I was all alone, begging for mercy while the thugs sharpened their knives. In one of my dreams, the Sacra Lista invaded Ralf's winery and shot my dad, who ended up sprawled on the floor in a pool of blood. I woke up in a cold sweat, trembling and shaking. During the day, I tried to read or write in my journal, but anxiety and dread colored my days a dark, ominous grey

An email arrived from Morgan that afternoon. I read it in a fog: *We're having a great time. Hope you are, too. Morgan.* I could hardly process what the message meant, it was so uncommunicative. What the heck did she mean? She didn't mention Italy, or ask any questions about what I was doing. I felt a knot in my stomach.

Finally, the day arrived when Carlo and his father were due to return from Napoli. I checked email obsessively all day, earning snickers from Carrie. Honestly, she was quite the pesky little sister but, I had to admit, our give-and-take was fun. In the late afternoon, Carlo's email showed up.

Alessandra, it read, *we must talk. I will pick you up at five. Carlo.*

My mouth went dry. Something was wrong. No terms of endearment. No *cara.* No *affezionatissimo.* What had happened? Had he found out that my dad was working on the Camorra investigation and he thought I was dishonest with him? Or had he decided to break up with me because he'd met some hot, sophisticated Italian girl in Napoli? Or was he going to end things because I was just an American tourist girl with whom he didn't have a chance for a long-term relationship?

The hands on my watch crawled toward five. I told Nicole and Phil that I might be gone for a while, perhaps even for dinner—I hoped. I felt deep down, however, that something had gone horribly wrong. I waited for Carlo outside the apartment. Given the terseness of Carlo's email, I thought it better not to put him in a situation that required social pleasantries.

"I'll see you later," I said to the Cowans, trying to sound cheerful.

"Those roses are beautiful," Nicole said, smiling.

The yellow roses were still blooming in my room. I had hoped that their long blooming was symbolic of my relationship with Carlo, but now I wasn't so sure.

I heard Carlo's Vespa before I saw it and took a deep breath. He roared up and wheeled around to face me. "Please, get on," he said, handing me the helmet, his face expressionless. I took it and climbed on the back.

No kiss, no embrace—no nothing.

Chapter Sixteen

We roared through the streets of Positano, climbing higher and higher, Carlo making dizzily sharp turns and skidding on the gravel. He didn't say a word, and I was afraid to break the silence. I clung to him, trying to feel his warmth, but he seemed cold and unapproachable. Finally, Carlo pulled the Vespa over at a turnout. He got off and abruptly motioned me to do likewise. I took off my helmet and slowly got off the Vespa. Below us lay the beautiful bay and the town of Positano. No one in the entire town knew what was going on up here, away from it all, I thought, fleetingly. Cars and motorcycles whizzed past us.

Carlo took off his helmet and looked at me with tears in his eyes. "Alessandra," he began. And then, in disbelief, I heard him say, "Or should I say, Alex?"

I felt suddenly cold.

"My father and I came home from Napoli to find our factory had been shut down. The inspectors came yesterday, and they found—how do you say, uncleanness? bacteria in the machines. They close us down and fine us."

"Oh, Carlo, I'm so sorry," I breathed, taking a step toward him.

Carlo held up his hand. "No, do not." He turned away from me, shoulders hunched and fists jammed in his pockets. "It is another way to try to get us to sell at a low price. But, there is more." He folded his arms, and I couldn't help but remember how those arms had once felt folding around me. "At the seminar, at the university, they are talking about American winemakers trying to break into the limoncello market here." He snorted in anger, his eyes flashing. "American winemakers know *nothing* about making limoncello. But who is here in Italy? Surprisingly, who is here, in Positano, right when all this is happening to our factory?" His jaw tightened and his eyes bore right through me.

"What?" I asked.

"Alex," he said—and the name cut right through me— "my father met with Giovanni LoPresti today. Giovanni told him that your family is trying to buy our factory and start distribution in the U.S. That it is *your* family behind the low offers and now the damage to the machines with the bacteria."

"But, Carlo—" I pleaded. My mind was numb and I felt as if I were underwater, trying desperately to reach the surface, to survive, to breathe. Stunned, I could only stare at his cold, implacable face. How could this be happening?

"You betrayed me, Alex," Carlo said, almost spitting out the words. "I became vulnerable to you. I let down my guard. And this is how you repaid me. You were here in Positano for a reason and you lied to me."

Chills swept over me. I could hardly believe what I was hearing. I burst into tears. "No, Carlo! It isn't true! My family...no one is involved in the limoncello factory! I swear it! And, honestly, I was going to tell you that my father is really trying to—"

In shock, I saw Carlo's face harden. He held up his hand, palm facing me. "Don't say any more. Giovanni told my father you would deny it. Your family lived too many years in Italy to not know how things work here, in the businesses. First the threats and intimidation and then the organized crime moves in. And your father and the knowing of the Italian language and working with the winery. My father was already questioning why you wanted the tour of our factory and then you take the pictures for your father as his spy. It is too perfect."

What could I say to him? Gulping for air, I clenched my hands into fists, trying to think clearly. What if I told him what I'd overheard today? Would he even listen?

"Carlo, I swear to you. I heard the *scugnizzi* talking about Giovanni wanting to move to the next level and they said he wanted to be an important man," I said, my words coming in bursts between sobs. "He's a criminal! He's going to be a *capo*! He's Sacra Lista!" I protested. "That's why he told you those things. They're not true!"

"How convenient you overheard that conversation," Carlo said, his voice cold as ice, his eyes frigid and his face impassive. "You remember how important my business is. I want to believe you"—and here, his voice broke, and he looked down at the ground. When he looked back up at me, I saw unshed tears glistening in his eyes—"but, too many things have fallen into place. My father warned me that we cannot trust anyone about our factory business, but I did not want to listen."

Carlo turned again to look out to sea. I wanted desperately to put my arms around him. In shock, I realized now why Giovanni and Signor LoPresti had been so interested in my father's work. It had nothing to do with Dad investigating the Camorra; it was because they were using me as a set-up, a smokescreen for the Sacra Lista's bid to take over Bertolucci Limoncello. What was I going to do? Would Carlo ever believe me?

"Carlo, please, I have to tell you—" I began.

Carlo folded his arms and shook his head. "I will not listen to your lies any more. I will take you home now, Alex," he said coldly. "I hope your family's winery is a success. But you will not buy us out. We will fix this."

It was agony to put my arms around him again, but I had to, just to hang on while we rode on the Vespa. My life was over. I couldn't believe what had just happened.

His back felt as hard and as unyielding as the conversation that had just passed between us. I had had a brief glimpse of tears in his eyes but now those tears, too, seemed unreal.

I tried desperately to keep some semblance of distance between us, but every time the Vespa zoomed around a corner, I was flung against Carlo's back, and I had to fight the impulse to cling to him. He didn't want to have anything to do with me now, and feeling my tears on his shirt would only make him even more furious.

We finally arrived at the apartment. Carlo didn't even turn

off the engine. Without a word, he held out his hand for the helmet. He looked at me with those eyes again. "Goodbye, Alex," he said in English.

Then, before I could answer, he revved the Vespa and zoomed off, without a backwards glance.

I felt as if I had been punched in the stomach. To gather some kind of calm before I had to face the Cowans, I leaned against the sun-warmed plaster wall. Carlo, Carlo, Carlo, I moaned silently. I'd let my guard down and I had let Italy become part of my heart again. Now I was accused of betrayal, even though it was *I* who had been betrayed— betrayed by Italy and its network of organized crime, but most of all, betrayed by my own self for not being honest. How I wished with all my heart that I had told Carlo about Dad earlier. This disaster would have been avoided. Tears filled my eyes, and I tried to hide my face from people walking by, fumbling in my bag in an attempt to find my keys.

Get it together, I scolded myself. I had to put on a brave face for the Cowans. I didn't want them to think that their super-nanny had gotten herself involved in something ugly. We had only two weeks left. I wondered if I could leave Italy early. I felt dismally that I didn't belong anywhere, that I didn't fit in with anyone, and that I was on a long and lonely path, all by myself. Truly, now I had no place to call my home. The U.S. had never been my home, and I saw that Italy truly had been—that is, until now.

Then, as I thought of what Giovanni had told the Bertoluccis—the accusation that I had deliberately and coldly

221

betrayed Carlo, and the lies about my father's sabotage—I was filled with fury. I wanted nothing more than to confront Giovanni. Imagining myself storming into the restaurant, confronting him in anger, watching him try to recover quickly and backpedal with his oh-so-charming manner gave me a small lift of hope. But then I shuddered a little, thinking of what the Sacra Lista did to people. I wondered if I had the courage to actually face Giovanni and tell him what I thought of him. The Sacra Lista and The System were formidable enemies. They routinely killed people without remorse, without compunction. Carlo's words echoed in my mind, "Remember, in Italy, some people think of the truth as that which gets you something."

A deep anger at Giovanni simmered within me, threatening to come to a boil. After I had decided to be completely honest with Carlo, I wasn't going to let Giovanni get away with telling lies about me. After a few minutes, I managed to calm my breathing, stop my tears, and take a ragged breath. Even if I managed to confront Giovanni successfully, I didn't know if Carlo would agree to see me again, and if he did, whether I could make him believe me. I remembered his cold and distant face, and knew the answer. Unless I could prove, somehow, that Dad and Ralf were not behind the sabotage and the low-priced offers, Carlo wouldn't believe anything I had to say to him. Giovanni and his father had been very clever, and I had been very stupid.

Now, though, I had to get off the street before any more people walked by me, saw my distraught condition and murmured, "*Poverina,*"— poor little girl, with an expression of genuine sympathy that you would never see on an American street; Americans would just avert their eyes. That didn't happen in Italy. I was dreading having to face the Cowans. If you ever wanted to put on a show, Alex, I told myself, this was the time.

Slowly, I walked up the stairs, making up a story that would forestall any questions they might have about Carlo. Carlo— his name caught in my throat along with the tears. This was the inevitable result of allowing myself to become Italian again, to merge, blend, and relax into the Italian landscape. I had been lulled by the beauty of Positano and tempted into a relationship with a gorgeous guy. Italia, for me, was nothing but hurt and heartbreak. I was so stupid, I scolded myself. If only I had known better than to let my heart rule my head.

Standing in front of the apartment door, I lifted my chin, put my shoulders back, and pasted a smile on my face. Hopefully, it wouldn't look too fake.

"Hi!" I said cheerfully, stepping into the living room. Nicole and Phil looked up from their reading, and Carrie looked up from the computer.

"Hi," Nicole said, looking surprised. "We thought you'd be gone through dinner."

"Well," I said, trying to sound positive, which was the very last thing I felt, "Carlo's business is in a bit of trouble right now and he has to work on that."

"So you won't be seeing him for a while?" Carrie asked. Even she looked concerned. Her twelve-year-old emotions had been tweaked by the romance of the story, the dinner dates, and the roses. I held back a sigh. So had *my* emotions. More than tweaked—overcome.

"No, I guess not," I said. "You know how Carlo is so focused on business." In fact, so focused on business that it took precedence over anything else, including the truth.

"Well, that's too bad," Phil said. "He was a nice young man."

"Yes, he was," Nicole affirmed.

They used the past tense, I noticed, which seemed only to cement my agony about what had just happened.

We took a shuttle up to the top of Positano for dinner, above the Nastro Azzurro, to another restaurant that our landlord had recommended. We zipped right past the turnout where Carlo had taken me earlier, and, unbidden, tears filled my eyes again.

Dinner was filled with talk of Saracens and Greeks and Normans, so, fortunately, all I was required to do was nod and agree and, every now and then, say, "Really?" Carrie was plugged into her iPhone. Honestly, I didn't know why Phil and Nicole let her get away with it so often, but then, conversation was much more pleasant for them when she was occupied and not complaining about everything; although, I had noticed her complaint level had dropped in the last couple of weeks. The magic of Italy had worked, even on Carrie, the unrepentant tweenager.

The lights of Positano winked up at me, the moon's glow shimmered across the flat expanse of the bay. It was a beautifully romantic night, which brought to mind my enchanted evening with Carlo. Tears came to my eyes again. Somewhere down there Carlo was thinking badly of me, thinking I had betrayed him. I could hardly bear the pain that stabbed through me at the thought. Devastated, I clenched my hands into fists in my lap and tried to control my emotions.

That evening, as soon as I turned out the light and slipped between the sheets, tears again began to roll down my cheeks and onto the pillow. Biting my tongue, I fought the sobs back, knowing Carrie would be all over me with questions, if she heard anything. My pain was private, my agony was real, and I didn't know what I could do about it. Hours seemed to drag by until I finally fell asleep just before dawn, tormented by dreams of Carlo. Even sleep offered no rest from my deep sadness.

It was early morning when I woke, and Carrie was still deeply asleep. In the mirror, I saw red, puffy eyes and quickly went into the bathroom to splash cold water on my face before anyone else woke up. Now, I would be counting the days down to my departure from Italy for a very different reason. It was time to turn my attention to America, to regroup and arm myself, so to speak, for the battle ahead— Sonoma. I'd email Morgan again, mentioning how much I missed all of them and the good old U.S. I shut my eyes for a moment. Then, I'd get back into my journal, writing as Alex, of course; although, I choked back a sob, I did not feel like Alex, not in the least. My emotions that tugged and pulled at me were telling me I was Alessandra.

Getting dressed quietly, I went into the living room. Phil was already up, drinking a cafe latte on the balcony.

"Well, good morning, Alessandra," he said, smiling.

I forced a smile. "Hi," I said.

"You're up early," Phil remarked. "Getting a little more rest without a boyfriend and all the late nights that go along with that?" he said. Then, as if he remembered what had happened, he quickly said, "I'm sorry. That was insensitive of me."

I smiled, certain that I must look like a death's mask. "No problem. Things happen," I said. Grabbing the Bialetti, I poured myself a coffee and added a little milk. "Do you mind if I use the computer?"

"No, go right ahead," Phil said.

Mom, Dad, and Sarah, another friend from Sonoma, had sent emails; none, however, from Morgan and none from Carlo. Clearing my throat, I answered them all.

Then, taking a deep breath, I wrote a cheery email to Morgan: *Hi from Italy! It's fun here, but I can't wait to get back and see you and everyone. I hope you had a great time in Tahoe and I'm sure sorry I missed it. I'll text you when I get back in two weeks. Heart, Alex.* I stared at the words and thought how false they were. False—just like Carlo thought *I* was. Clicking *send*, I turned off the computer with a sigh.

After everyone else woke up and we discussed the day's activities—a possible walk for Carrie and me, and work for Nicole and Phil—I sat on the balcony, reading and writing in my journal, trying not to listen to the Italian on the street below me. What was Giovanni going to do in the Sacra Lista? How *could* he have suggested that my father was involved in the Bertolucci factory buy-out, and that *I* was part of the conspiracy? Anger filled me once again at the injustice of his lies. I felt a growing rage at the betrayal and the ugliness of it all. I balled my hands involuntarily into fists. It just wasn't fair—and I didn't know what I could do about it. As I tried to take a deep breath and relax into my chair, I realized my teeth were clenched, my muscles tight. I realized that I would have to handle this problem with Giovanni or it would haunt me forever.

"I'm bored," Carrie called from the computer. "Want to go on a walk?"

"Sure," I said. We'd been going on long walks every other day or so. Carrie loved looking at the Italian guys and, until now, I had loved soaking up the Italian atmosphere; the sights, sounds, and smells—everything that I knew would be lost to me once I went back to the U.S. Now, I simply felt tired of it all and longed for the day that the plane would whisk me away forever.

"Oh, wait!" Carrie exclaimed from the computer. "I just got an email from Ben!" She sounded excited and I had to smile, in spite of myself. "They're leaving late today and want to meet us for lunch. Can we, Dad?"

"Sure," Phil said.

"How about the delicatessen, down by La Spiaggia Grande?" I said. "The guy will fix us *panini* and we can eat

227

them at the *piazzola* on the way to Il Torre Clavel."

"Great!" Carrie said, bouncing up and down in excitement. Her fingers clicked a happy response over the keyboard.

"Ready to go?" Carrie asked me, after jumping up from the desk.

"Uh-huh," I replied, looking up from my journal. I put my journal back in my bedroom drawer and grabbed my shoes from the wardrobe. Carrie probably had a lot of questions for me, questions about Carlo that she probably guessed I didn't want to answer. She had kept her questions to herself, so far anyway. I wondered whether she was finally growing up a little. At least one of us was blooming in the warm Italian sun.

Shouldering my bag and grabbing a bottle of water, I opened the door for Carrie and felt the warmth of Italy wrap itself around me. the sun was bright, the pedestrians chattered on the street in their musical Italian, the purple and red bougainvillea climbed the ancient walls, and the geraniums and rosemary bloomed in window boxes. Carlo, Carlo, I thought. I drew a ragged breath and brushed tears from my eyes before Carrie could see.

We began our walk the usual way, down Via Vicolo Vito Savino toward the LoPrestis' restaurant, where everything was closed and shuttered at this early hour.

Carrie glanced over at the restaurant and sighed a little. I snorted.

"What?" she demanded, scuffing her shoes on the pavement.

"He is just trouble," I said, deciding to leave it there.

Actually, I wanted to kick at the metal shutters that covered the front entrance and yell at Giovanni for being so hateful. He had ruined everything for me—Carlo, Italy, my entire life. I felt that I had to do something, but didn't know exactly what. I still could not comprehend that Giovanni, who had seemed so nice, was such a liar, and that Carlo had so readily believed his lies.

I knew that the last months of my life in Sonoma had also been built on lies. In becoming Alex, I had shut out Alessandra. I had wanted to fit in so much with my new friends that I had completely blocked out who I really was and lied to them and to myself.

Now, Giovanni had lied about me and I was furious. I didn't care about the price I would have to pay, not now. I'd already lost Carlo and had nothing left to lose. I felt my eyes well up with tears again and brushed my hand across them. No more lies for me. Besides, the Sacra Lista wouldn't bother killing a stupid American teenager. The international attention brought about by such a murder would result in a bright light being shone on the Sacra Lista, which is the last thing they would want. I was going to take care of this problem once and for all. No unspoken code of *omerta* was going to stop me. No liar was going to stand there and call *me* a liar!

Carrie chattered on about everything she saw as we walked past the shops. "Alessandra, look at that really cute blue dress with the lemons on the skirt hanging in the doorway! Oh, look at these sandals," she exclaimed, stopping in front of a store's display tables. "These rings are beautiful!" she cried, holding up a sterling silver ring embossed with lemons.

Luckily, all she required from me was an "Uh-huh," and "Yes," because my thoughts were elsewhere. Now I knew why people wrote about a broken heart—it truly did feel broken. I'd never felt such a real connection with any guy before. Carlo had called me his "soul-mate," and that was how I felt about him too. If only I'd told him the truth about Dad's investigations.

"Wait," Carrie said, stopping in front of another shop. "I want to see that bathing suit." I followed her in, greeted the shopkeeper, and sat on a bench while she went through the bikinis on a rack. I just didn't have the heart to shop. I didn't even have a heart—it had been shattered.

Carrie picked out several bikinis to try on and vanished behind one of the curtains. In my mind, I went over what I would say to Giovanni. Things were over with Carlo—I couldn't erase the sight of his cold, accusing eyes—but at least I could stand up for myself, for once, and call Giovanni a liar to his face. I was going to lay it all out for him, no more niceties, no more ignoring reality. It probably wouldn't make a bit of difference to Giovanni, but it would make a big difference to me.

The Indiana kids beat us to the delicatessen, and were trying to make themselves understood to the guy behind the counter. I did not recognize the employee, even though we had been to the delicatessen to eat lots of times before.

"Hey!" Carrie said, delightedly. The kids were happy and relieved to see us.

"Thank God you're here," Georgia said. "I can't explain what I want."

After the usual polite pleasantries in Italian with the deli guy, I told him what everyone wanted to eat.

"*Di dov'è Lei, Signorina?*" he asked, curiously. Where are you from?

I smiled and opened my mouth to answer. Then, suddenly, it hit me. For too long, I had thought that, in order to be like everyone else in Sonoma, I needed to completely forget Italy and be only and always American. These last weeks in Italy had taught me that maybe, just maybe, I could belong to *both* worlds—Italy and the U.S. My inside self could be my outside self, too. Finally.

"*Sono Americana, ma, quando ero più giovane, ho abitato in Italia,*" I said. "*Sono tutte le due.*" I am American, but when I was younger, I lived in Italy. I am both.

"*Ah, sì! Bene!*" he said, grinning.

Our *panini* in paper bags, we began walking to La Spiaggia Fornillo. I remembered the last time we were here, on the beach with Carlo. I shut my eyes for a second, willing the tears not to come. Carlo had met the other factory owner, Signor Scioscia, on this tourist path. They had discussed the difficulties of the Bertolucci factory, the insidious, low-priced offers. The tentacles of the Sacra Lista and the Camorra, and of all the organized crime families, were wound around and through the lives of Italians. Some few strong individuals were able to break free, but it required courage, resourcefulness, knowing the right people in government, negotiating, and, ultimately, standing up for what was right. Knowing Carlo and his family, I felt certain that the Bertoluccis would be able to do that.

Then the thought occurred to me: Maybe I could help them do it. But now, the Bertoluccis would have nothing to do with me, after Giovanni's accusations. That shouldn't prevent me from doing the right thing, though, I vowed to myself.

Ahead of us, at the end of the cliff, I saw Il Torre Clavel, standing guard as it had for centuries. Some things about Italy never changed. The people were unfailingly kind; their love of life, and their willingness to let people live their own lives was a part of Italy that I had always cherished. Italy was an important part of who I was, who I had become, and no one was going to steal that from me, not Giovanni, not my new American friends, no one.

We sat on stone benches by the little *piazzola*, and the four kids laughed and talked together, making plans to stay in touch once they got back to the U.S. Carrie told them how great California was and how they needed to come and visit her there.

"Well, we like Indiana, but it doesn't have anything on California," Hayley said, making a face.

"It's fine, and we have some fun times," Georgia said defensively.

"Good sports teams," Ben said.

"What?" both girls said in unison, and then everyone laughed.

"Well," Ben said, his face a little red, "good state teams, anyway."

Listening to them defend their home states, I was glad I didn't have to join in. In spite of my realization that I wasn't really looking forward to going back to the States and to my life in California, I had decided to try this being-part-of-both-worlds out and see how it worked.

First, I was going to talk with Giovanni and set him straight. Then, I'd try to contact the Bertoluccis to see if I could help them in their fight against the Sacra Lista.

Regardless of what Carlo thought of me, I knew that I couldn't leave Italy without trying to make things right for Carlo, his family—and myself.

Chapter Eighteen

The afternoon wore on. The Indiana kids had brought two packs of cards and taught Carrie and me a game called *Golf*, where you could try to psych out the other players. At least they weren't doing crazy stuff like trying to balance on the parapet of Il Torre Clavel with the waves crashing far below. I'd have to play lifeguard then, and that didn't appeal to me. Emotionally, I was exhausted, and the image of Carlo with his shirtsleeves rolled up and the ocean breeze ruffling his hair was real and raw in my mind.

The sun dropped lower in the sky, sending a greenish-blue reflection across the water. Finally, I looked at my watch and, playing the nanny once again, said, "Okay, kids. Time to go. We have to get ready for dinner and you guys are leaving. Your parents are probably wondering where you are."

With groans and complaints, they picked up the cards, and we walked back across the walkway to La Spiaggia Fornillo, across the wharf to La Spiaggia Grande, and up the main street back into town.

The four kids hugged farewell with tears and giggles and promises to text.

"Goodbye!"

"*Arrivederci!*"

"Thanks for helping us with Italy," Georgia said, which

made my eyes sting with unshed tears.

Waving until we couldn't see them anymore, Carrie and I trudged up the streets to the apartment. I had to admit, I was looking for Carlo everywhere. Did I see him in the crowd on La Spiaggia? Was he cruising around the corner on his Vespa? Was he in one of the limoncello shops, arranging another delivery? My heart ached. How could something that was supposed to be just a functioning organ in my body, pumping blood through my veins and arteries, be a source of so much pain?

The moment I had dreaded all day was now approaching. We were passing Café LoPresti and, sure enough, Carrie slowed up. Just as she did so, a kid on a Vespa almost hit us, reaching out to grab Carrie's bag as he swerved past. He gave a violent yank on the bag slung over Carrie's shoulder, throwing her off her feet. Carrie fell screaming to the pavement, still clutching her bag. The kid zoomed off, empty-handed, little curls of exhaust hanging in the air.

"Oh, my God!" Carrie shrieked.

People stood shocked and motionless, then moved on, almost at the same time. Italian mingled with English and German as people bent over Carrie, helping her to her feet. It had all happened so fast that I could hardly register that it had happened at all.

Carrie's arms and face were bruised and scraped, and she moaned tearfully about her shoulder. I gave her a hug and she sniffled into my shoulder. A *nonna* pulled a white handkerchief from her purse and mopped at Carrie's brow, murmuring, "*Poverina, poverina mia.*"

Someone offered to get an ambulance but I could see it wasn't necessary. Carrie just needed to get home to her mom and dad. Suddenly, I realized I felt like her big sister, not her nanny.

"*Carabinieri,*" someone said. "*Li chiamo.*"

"*Non é necessario chiamare i carabinieri,*" I heard a voice say over my shoulder.

Looking up, I saw Giovanni. No wonder you don't think we need to call the *carabinieri*, you lousy jerk, I thought. They're the last people *you'd* want around here. My heart rate accelerated with suppressed anger.

Carrie stood beside me as two Italian women mopped her brow and massaged her shoulders. Her tear-streaked face was white, but her wails had quietened to sniffles and whimpers. She was going to be fine.

I stood up, squarely facing Giovanni. A sardonic smile lingered on his face, as he stood with one hand on his hip. I felt a rush of anger, the like of which I had never felt before, and it channeled fiercely into my Italian self.

"You!" I spat in Italian. "You dare to even use the word *carabinieri*? You slimeball! You, who think nothing of betraying someone! You have no business even taking a breath!"

The crowd around us fell silent—even people who weren't Italian and couldn't understand what I was saying could sense that something serious was happening.

For an instant, Giovanni's face looked shocked, before a

calculating, cold expression molded his features. "You are a stupid girl," he said, condescendingly. He looked around the small crowd, almost as if asking for confirmation as to the stupidity of American girls. "You don't even know what you're talking about. You do not know what you are dealing with here."

My breath seemed to come in gasps, but I forced myself to go on. I was shaking with fury. "My family and the Bertolucci factory! Does that sound familiar?" I cried. "You are a liar! We had *nothing* to do with it! Nothing!" I was making a scene in the street but I didn't care. I'd lost Carlo and it was Giovanni's fault. From the corner of my eye, I saw Carrie's white face, eyes wide, staring at me. A side of Alessandra she had not seen before, I thought grimly.

"I don't know what you're talking about," Giovanni said arrogantly. He tried to play to the crowd, shrugging and turning his palms upward.

"You know exactly what I'm talking about, you jerk," I spat.

"If you mean the factory, well then, that's the way it is here," he said calmly. Then he laughed. "You have to understand, you Americans, that here, the truth is only what gets you something."

The small crowd murmured at that, and I was sure from their reactions that even the Italians didn't completely agree with Giovanni's statement.

"*You* are behind the conspiracy. It is you and the Sacra Lista." Behind me, I could sense the crowd shrinking back from us. The dreaded phrase had done its work.

Giovanni snorted. "Sacra Lista. Those are only words. You are only a girl, and an American girl, and you have no idea about the meaning of those words."

Suddenly, another voice spoke from behind me. It was Carlo!

"I have words for you, Giovanni," Carlo said evenly. I whipped around to see Carlo, standing with his arms folded, his head to the side, staring at Giovanni as if he were examining an ugly biological specimen under a slide.

"You!" Giovanni laughed, but I could see his demeanor was cracking. He was rubbing his thumbs nervously against his forefingers.

"Yes, I," Carlo said. He moved past me, without looking at me, and stood before Giovanni, who took a step back. "I will defeat you," Carlo said. "And that is not a threat. I do not deal in threats. That is a promise."

"You are challenging the wrong man," Giovanni protested.

"No," Carlo said, quietly, staring into Giovanni's eyes. "*You* are challenging the wrong man." Then Carlo glanced at me, and my heart stopped for an instant before he turned back to Giovanni. "This is only the beginning."

"We shall see," Giovanni blustered, gesturing to the small crowd that had fallen silent. Even Carrie's sobs were muted. "We shall see." He stalked back to his restaurant.

Everyone began talking at once, solicitously hovering over Carrie, some clapping Carlo on the back, others patting me on the shoulder. I stood still, staring at Carlo. His deep brown eyes gazed into mine. Then, he smiled—that smile that lit up his face and crinkled the corners of his eyes. Carlo took a step toward me, his hands outstretched, and I fell into his arms. His strong arms encircled me and his lips brushed mine.

"*Carissima*," he breathed in my ear, "I am so sorry."

"But—but, how did you know?" I asked.

He put his finger gently across my lips. "Shhhh," he whispered. "One of the new workers was bribed by the Sacra Lista to put the bacteria on the machines. He confessed today."

"How—why?" I asked.

Carlo smiled. "Let's just say that I have a talent for the business," he said. "I knew the questions to ask everyone and how to ask them."

"So you know Giovanni lied to you?" I asked.

Carlo tipped my face back and kissed me full on the lips. Some in the audience tittered and some clapped. The little group was dispersing, but some had stayed, no doubt, to watch the concluding drama of the love story. Carrie was being attended to by the little *nonna*, and she looked as if she was recovering nicely.

"You, *carissima*, are my soul-mate, and I should have known it in my heart from the beginning. I was coming here to tell Giovanni what I had learned, and I came upon this scene," he said, running his fingers through my hair. "You are a brave one, Alessandra." He kissed me again, and I melted into his arms.

A brave one, he had said. Well, I guessed that was true. I would see how brave I could be when it came time to go back to the U.S., but I thought now that I could do it. I wasn't going to lie about *Italia* any more, and whatever Morgan and my new friends thought about it would be just fine. Italy was too much a part of me to pretend anything different any longer. I was who I was, and I was finally proud of it.

"And I think I know what you were going to tell me about your father," Carlo said softly in my ear. "We heard rumors during the seminar that some people in a California winery were trying to find out which Italian wineries were controlled by the Camorra."

Relief washed over me. He would believe me, after all! "My dad told me not to tell anyone, but I really wanted to let you know—and I was going to," I said, my words tumbling over each other. "I'm so sorry." Tears filled my eyes. "Oh, Carlo, I've made a mess of everything—here and back in California."

"You will triumph, Alessandra," Carlo said. "You will be fine back in the U.S. I know it. We will take care of this problem here first, together. And we will be together in so many ways, for so many years. I have plans."

"Alessandra!" Carrie interrupted. "Let's go home. I need some Band-Aids!"

"I have to go now." I smiled at Carlo through our kisses.

"Tonight, dinner, nine. I will call for you," he said. "We will talk about when to meet with the police and some government officials, along with Signor Scioscia and my parents, and give Giovanni an ugly surprise he will not forget. The truth *will* get us something. It will get Giovanni and his truth-loving friends a number of years in an Italian prison." He smiled into my eyes. "Oh, and we will talk about how possibly I will study viticulture in California next year at the university close to where you live."

"In California? Really?" My heart filled with a rush of joy, and I hugged him, hard, luxuriating in the feel of his strong back under his starched shirt. We could be together next year!

"Alessandra!" Carrie grumbled. "Enough of the smooching! I'm bleeding!"

"Nine, then?" he said, grinning, as he released me. "I'll call for you at nine."

"You can call for me, and you can call me Alessandra," I said, "forever."

Acknowledgements

In grateful acknowledgment for all you have done for this manuscript; this book could not have been written without your invaluable help: Bonnie, Carmela, Gabriele, James and Manuela, Katie, Nicki and Mariana, Margherita, and Jaynie.

CPSIA information can be obtained
at www.ICGtesting.com
Printed in the USA
FSHW010637051118
53554FS